Garden
OF
Graves

Garden OF Graves

THE SHOCKING TRUE STORY OF LONG ISLAND SERIAL KILLER JOEL RIFKIN

MARIA EFTIMIADES

ST. MARTIN'S PAPERBACKS

Acknowledgments

My sincere thanks to *People* Managing Editor Landon Y. Jones for his continued patience and support. It has been most appreciated.

Also, thanks are due to my editors, Assistant Managing Editor Cutler Durkee, Chief of Correspondents Maria Wilhelm, Senior Editor Jack Friedman, and Senior Editor Joe Treen.

As always, I am grateful to Charles Spicer and the gang at St. Martin's, and my agent, Jane Dystel.

Chapter 1

IN the predawn mist, the headlights on the 1984 gray Mazda SE pickup cast an eerie glow as the truck pulled away from 1492 Garden Street. No one saw the driver as he turned down Spruce Lane and inched his way to Bellmore Avenue, heading south. If anyone had, they probably wouldn't have been surprised. In this middle-class neighborhood of East Meadow, Long Island, neighbors were accustomed to seeing the Mazda coming and going at odd hours.

The driver was tired. His face was smudged, his jeans and red flannel shirt stained. For the last hour, he'd been loading heavy cargo in the back of the pickup. He'd had to lift a bundle out of a wheelbarrow stored in the garage. A few days earlier, he'd wrapped the cargo in a blue tarpaulin, deftly fastening a heavy cord. He was getting pretty good at securing his load. Recently he'd bought a book called *Ropes & Knots*. Alone in his bedroom at night, he practiced.

When the tarp was prepared, the driver turned a lever to open the cap cover of the pickup and dropped the tailgate. It took a while to hoist the tarp inside. The cargo was particularly heavy that night.

The driver tried to be quiet as he went about his work. It didn't really matter. Inside 1492 Garden Street his mother and sister slept soundly. Besides, the driver suspected they would not question him if they heard him rummaging in the garage long past midnight. They seldom questioned him about anything at all.

It was 3:15 A.M. New York State Trooper Deborah Spaargaren pointed the navy patrol car with yellow stripes east on the Southern State Parkway. Spaargaren and her partner, Trooper Sean Ruane, were midway through their 11:00 P.M. to 7 A.M. shift, patrolling the parkways of Nassau and Suffolk counties on Long Island. Under state trooper safety

2

guidelines, they patrolled together until dawn, then alone until the shift ended. Tonight, the patrol was relatively quiet. Sundays usually were.

Spaargaren and Ruane were among the youngest troopers on the force. Spaargaren, twenty-three, had joined the state troopers fifteen months earlier. Ruane, twenty-five, had three years on the job. Already, Ruane had earned his share of accolades. In 1991 he stopped a murder suspect on a road in Sullivan County, not far from Kiamesha Lake, where a Hasidic couple had been brutally slain. The following year the young cop apprehended two convicted killers after they'd escaped from an upstate penitentiary.

Spaargaren and Ruane were among the forty-three hundred state troopers who patrol the highways and parkways in the sixty-two counties of New York State. They were committed to law enforcement.

So when they spotted the Mazda a few hundred yards before the Wantagh exit on the parkway, they observed it with trained eyes. Its speed didn't concern the young cops. The pickup was traveling a few miles above New York State's fifty-five-mile-an-hour speed limit—hardly fast enough to inspire the troopers to issue a summons.

What caught their attention, however, was the back of the truck. Above the bumper, where the license plate should have been, there was nothing.

Driving without a license plate is a minor traffic violation. Still, it wasn't something state troopers overlooked. Especially troopers like Spaargaren and Ruane.

The partners didn't hesitate. Ruane leaned over and snapped the switch activating the red lights atop the roof rack. The lights began to flash. Spaargaren sped up slightly, positioning the patrol car directly behind the Mazda.

The driver of the pickup stole a quick glance in his rearview mirror. His hands clenched the steering wheel a bit tighter. His foot never left the accelerator.

It took a minute before the troopers realized the driver of the pickup had no intention of pulling over. He didn't go faster. He didn't change lanes. He simply continued to drive, seemingly oblivious of the swirling red lights atop patrol car No. 1L35.

Ruane tried again. He activated the siren. It fractured the deadly quiet of the late hour.

But the driver showed no reaction. The pickup continued at a steady clip.

Ruane reached for the loudspeaker portion of the radio. He keyed the mike. His voice resonated along the parkway, tight with anger.

"Pull over to the side of the road," Ruane demanded.

Again, no reaction. The troopers glanced at each other, uneasy. This was turning out to be much more than a routine traffic stop. No doubt, the driver of the pickup had something to hide.

Ruane reached again for the radio. He called in a report to the sergeant on duty in the communications section of state trooper headquarters, Troop L, in East Farmingdale.

"Car 1L35 to Farmingdale," Ruane said.

The trooper gave a terse description of the situation: Driver, male. Operating a gray Mazda pickup. No plate. Refuses repeated orders to pull over. 1L35 requests backup. Ruane signed off with his shield number.

Headquarters reacted swiftly. Within minutes, three state trooper cars were dispatched to join the chase. The sergeant on duty at the command post also notified Nassau County police. They, too, sent officers to the scene.

Despite the growing police convoy behind him, the driver of the Mazda appeared nonplussed as he continued east on the Southern State Parkway. Then, without warning, he veered to the right, speeding up the off-ramp of exit 28 in Wantagh. Ignoring the stop sign at the top of the hill, the driver sailed down Wantagh Avenue, angling north.

For the next ten minutes, the driver snaked through back roads in residential neighborhoods, trying to shake the cops. It was useless; they were directly behind him. When he reached Old Country Road in Mineola, a busy thoroughfare, the driver made a choice. After a moment's delay, he swerved the truck sharply to the right, rounding the corner of Washington Avenue and Old Country Road.

He swung too wide. The Mazda crashed into a wooden light pole, knocking it to the ground and shattering glass all over the sidewalk. The driver was thrown back in his seat, his hands still gripping the steering wheel.

Behind him, at least half a dozen police cars screeched to a halt. In seconds, a team of state troopers and Nassau County cops encircled the pickup.

The driver did not move. Through the trees, in the darkness of the early morning, he could see lights blazing in front of the Nassau County Criminal Courthouse half a block away.

Trooper Ruane reached the truck first. Revolver poised, he peered into the cab. With his free hand, he opened the door.

"Get out," he barked.

Joel Rifkin did as he was told. He climbed out, hands raised. Without being asked, he lay facedown on the pavement, arms and legs spread. Troopers frisked him. They found nothing—no weapons, no drugs. It seemed odd. What did Joel Rifkin have to hide?

One trooper suspected he knew the answer. In fact, every cop at the scene did too. There was an odor emanating from the back of the pickup. A pungent odor. A familiar odor.

The cops exchanged glances. The trooper broke the silence. He motioned to the back of the pickup. He looked directly into Joel Rifkin's steel gray eyes.

"Smells like you got a body back there," the trooper said quietly.*

Joel Rifkin stared straight ahead.

---

*The police later denied they said this.

Chapter 2

TROOPERS handcuffed Joel Rifkin and led him to a patrol car, ordering him to sit in the back. He showed no emotion as they arrested him and read him his rights.

Meanwhile, Spaargaren and Ruane remained with the pickup. They unlocked the tailgate, dropped it, and peered inside, shining flashlights from top to bottom. The blue tarpaulin filled the bed of the truck. Using the tips of their flashlights, the troopers cautiously lifted a corner of the tarp. The smell grew even more potent. They lifted the edge of the tarp a little higher. Their suspicions were promptly confirmed.

Inside the tarp was the decomposing body

of a woman. From the looks of the body and its stench, the cops guessed she'd been dead a few days. They shone a flashlight onto her face. For a moment, no one spoke.

The troopers didn't know they were looking at the body of Tiffany Bresciani, that she had been just twenty-two years old, a pretty, petite aspiring writer from Metairie, Louisiana. They didn't know that for the past few days Tiffany's mother, Cheryl, had been worried about her only child. Since Tiffany moved to New York City several years earlier, she'd always called home frequently.

But there had been no phone call since Thursday, June 24. Late that night, three days before police would spot the Mazda pickup on the parkway, Cheryl Bresciani's only child had made a terrible mistake: she'd climbed into a car with Joel Rifkin.

By 3:30 A.M. more than a dozen state troopers and Nassau County cops were swarming along the corner of Old Country Road and Washington Avenue. They cordoned off the area and examined the interior of the pickup, strewn with trash. Their findings were disturbing. A pair of women's shoes. Gray stretch tights with one pink sock attached. A pair of rubber gloves. A wooden handled steak knife. On the dashboard in the cab, a Grateful Dead sticker. On the back bumper, another sticker: STICKS AND STONES MAY BREAK MY BONES BUT WHIPS AND CHAINS EXCITE ME.

The troopers studied Joel Rifkin's driver's license: "Rifkin, Joel D. 1492 Garden Street, East Meadow, New York 11554. Eyes: gray. Height: 5 ft. 10. Born 01/20/59. Wears corrective lenses."

But the cops respectfully stepped aside to allow Ruane and Spaargaren to question the suspect. Joel Rifkin was, after all, caught because of the tenacity of the young cops.

The troopers asked the obvious question. Who was the woman in the truck?

Joel Rifkin answered without hesitating, his voice composed.

"She was a prostitute," he said. "I had sex with her, and then I killed her."

The troopers were stunned. A minor traffic infraction had somehow spiraled into a murder case. And the suspect didn't seem the least perturbed. Outside the patrol car, Spaargaren and Ruane consulted briefly. It was definitely time to radio headquarters with the latest developments.

News traveled fast. Troopers on overnight duty in East Farmingdale immediately telephoned several senior investigators at home. Details were still sketchy, they explained. But there was a suspect, an East Meadow man who'd confessed to killing a woman. Perhaps there was even more to this grisly story. The detectives didn't need urging. They hurried to headquarters at once.

Once the detectives were on their way, the troopers consulted a list to find out which assistant district attorney from the Major Offenses Bureau was on call for the week. Six ADAs worked for Nassau County District Attorney Denis Dillon. Each took turns manning the bureau a week at a time.

Assistant District Attorney Fred Klein's shift was due to end at 9:00 A.M. Monday morning. But five hours before it did, Joel Rifkin was apprehended with a body in his truck. Klein got the case.

Since joining the DA's office in 1978, Fred Klein had been one of the more valued ADAs on Long Island. He was aggressive and tenacious. And he'd had a good deal of experience dealing with the media.

In recent months Klein had wrapped the most infamous case of his career—the prosecution of Amy Fisher, the Long Island teenager who had shot her alleged lover's wife in the head. The assistant district attorney loathed the publicity the story had engendered. Ducking interviews, he'd tried to focus on the case. After six months, Klein had negotiated a plea bargain with Fisher's attorney. When the Long Island teen was finally sentenced to five to fifteen years in prison and sent to an upstate New York prison in December 1992, Fred Klein was relieved.

But it wasn't over. Two months later, DA Dillon had assigned Klein to an equally high profile case—the prosecution of Joey Buttafuoco, Amy's alleged lover, on statutory rape charges.

So when the telephone rang a few hours before his shift was scheduled to end, Fred Klein could only wonder what was in store for him next.

Klein listened as troopers explained the situation. A man. A body. A confession. Klein dressed quickly and drove straight to Mineola.

It was shortly before 4:00 A.M. The patrol car carrying Joel Rifkin, its lights flashing, sped down the Southern State Parkway. It was important to bring the accused in for interrogation as soon as possible. The patrol car raced past the spot where Spaargaren and Ruane had first signaled the pickup to pull over, less than an hour before.

In the car, Joel Rifkin responded to troopers' questions effortlessly. He told them he was a landscaper, but that he hadn't worked in some time. Now and then he did office temp work for various companies on Long Island. He was thirty-four years old, an East Meadow resident. He lived at home with his mother, Jeanne, and sister, Jan. His father, Bernard, had died six years ago.

Without much coaxing, Joel Rifkin began to volunteer details on the murder. He told the troopers that on Thursday evening he'd borrowed his mother's 1986 blue Toyota four-door sedan and driven to Manhattan. For a while, he'd cruised Allen Street on the Lower East Side, one of his favorite haunts, as well as Twelfth Street and Second Avenue in the East Village. Both areas are known to be frequented by prostitutes.

Rifkin spotted Tiffany Bresciani on Canal Street. She'd been working the street off and on for several years. She wore a simple black skirt and a green blouse. She had a couple of tattoos—one of a purple rose encircling her left wrist and an ankh symbol—the Egyptian symbol for life—on a floral background on her left hip.

Like almost every prostitute on the streets of New York City, Tiffany Bresciani was a drug addict. For several years heroin had been her drug of choice. But lately, Bresciani had been fighting her disease. She'd joined a methadone program in the city. Every day, she got her daily fix of the orange liquid.

But in a short time she was back walking the streets, selling her body to get high. It was an existence she loathed, a world away from life as Cheryl Bresciani's little girl in Metairie. But like so many others, Tiffany Bresciani felt powerless. The lure of drugs was formidable.

So when Joel Rifkin rolled down his window late Thursday night and motioned, Tiffany Bresciani willingly responded. She walked over to the Toyota and leaned in. It only took a minute to negotiate a price: forty or fifty dollars was standard. It would be enough for the evening's high. And so Tiffany Bresciani, whose grandmother called her "little lamb," got in the passenger seat of Joel Rifkin's car and pulled the door shut.

Rifkin drove just a few hundred yards, parking the Toyota in an isolated spot near the Manhattan Bridge. It wasn't unusual for prostitutes and their clients to conduct business around the bridge. Between drug sales and prostitution, the area is often jammed with cars. Now and then, New York City cops sweep the site, arresting dozens of hookers and loading them into a van.

But no one was around the night Joel Rifkin took Tiffany Bresciani under the shadow of the Manhattan Bridge. No one heard her muffled gasps. No one was there to save her. Rifkin told police that as he began having sex with Tiffany Bresciani he placed his hands around her neck. As her eyes widened with terror, he squeezed with all his force. In just a minute, Tiffany Bresciani was dead.

Joel Rifkin looked at her for a long time. She had been an attractive girl. Such lovely reddish brown hair.

Back in Metairie, Tiffany's mother and grandmother waited for a telephone call. Earlier, they'd mailed a care package to Tiffany filled with summer dresses, pictures, and a white teddy bear.

Tiffany's boyfriend, Rick Wilder, was also waiting. The two had lived together off and on for several years. Tiffany's drug problem caused a strain on the relationship. But

Rick, a rock musician and aspiring actor, loved Tiffany. And she loved him.

With Tiffany Bresciani's body beside him, Joel Rifkin started the engine of his mother's Toyota. He cruised past the prostitutes and drug addicts on Canal Street. Tiffany's friends on the strip were still working. They wouldn't begin to miss her for several days.

Joel Rifkin left Manhattan and drove to Levittown, not far from his East Meadow home. He bought the blue tarp and yards of heavy cord. In a secluded parking lot he painstakingly wrapped Tiffany's body and dragged it from the car seat to the trunk.

Joel Rifkin drove home and slept for a long time. It had been a busy night.

The day after he killed Tiffany Bresciani, Joel Rifkin moved her body to a wheelbarrow in the detached garage next to his mother's home. Sooner or later, Jeanne Rifkin would need the Toyota. Leaving a body in the back wasn't a good idea.

Rifkin wasn't sure what to do about the bloodstains on the upholstery and in the trunk. He shrugged it off. He had never been questioned before.

Leaving the body in the garage was a problem, however. In the heat of the summer, it would decompose rapidly. Neighbors might complain about the smell and start asking questions. Rifkin knew he had to act quickly. So early Monday morning he set out for Republic Airport, about ten miles from East Meadow. The fields and bushes surrounding the runways would be a good place to dump a body. Ideal, in fact.

Joel Rifkin confessed his plan not long after he was collared by police. The troopers couldn't help but catch the irony; Republic Airport, on Route 110 in East Farmingdale, is adjacent to state trooper headquarters. In his final act of bravado, Joel Rifkin had intended to discard the body of Tiffany Bresciani only a few hundred yards from an area rife with cops.

Shortly after Joel Rifkin arrived at headquarters, he met with Senior Investigator Tom Capers and Investigator Steve Louder. The three men faced off in a small room. Capers and Louder were skilled interviewers. Capers had been a detective for fifteen years; Louder, ten. Both men understood the intricacies of obtaining information. They knew they had to ensure that Joel Rifkin felt comfortable. They had to gain his trust.

It is customary for only one or two detectives to interrogate a suspect; it makes it more likely the suspect will speak freely. Besides, if there are too many interviewers, a savvy defense attorney could claim the suspect had been badgered into a confession. In the case of Joel Rifkin, state troopers were taking no chances.

Despite the facts—that a young woman was found dead in Joel Rifkin's truck—Capers and Louder approached the East Meadow man gently, in an almost fraternal manner. They knew the drill; the more at ease a suspect felt, the more likely he'd offer details about his crime.

For the next few hours the investigators learned all they could about Joel Rifkin and the murder of Tiffany Bresciani. The landscaper told them he had been going to prostitutes two or three times a week since he earned his New York State driver's license at age eighteen. Rifkin frequently used the word "patronizing" when talking about his late-night forays into lower Manhattan, looking for a woman. He said he'd "patronized" Tiffany Bresciani. He described the "date"—how he'd approached the young woman on Canal Street, and how they'd agreed on a price for sex. With his hands, Joel Rifkin demonstrated what he had done to Cheryl Bresciani's only child.

He told the detectives where he'd bought the tarp and cord. He explained that he had used his mother's car, and that he was forced to move the body to the garage and then to the pickup before he attempted to dispose of it.

By dawn, the investigators knew enough to determine that the local media would likely take great interest in this story. It had all the elements: A quiet landscaper from a middle-class neighborhood. A dead prostitute in the back of a pickup. A high speed chase. Two young hero cops.

Troopers prepared a one-page press release. The investigators reviewed it and gave it their okay. It read:

New York State troopers are investigating the circumstances surrounding the death of a white female discovered in a pickup truck following a vehicle and traffic stop at 4 a.m. this morning, June 28, 1993, in Nassau County, N.Y.

Two troopers on patrol of the Southern State Parkway in Nassau County attempted to stop a male operator for a traffic violation early this morning. The driver would not stop and troopers pursued the pickup onto Wantagh Avenue North and then onto Old Country Road West. The pickup eventually collided with a light pole at Old Country Road and Washington Avenue in Mineola. At the scene, troopers discovered the body of a white female in the back of the pickup. The driver has been arrested and state police investigators will be available to address questions concerning this case at approximately 1 p.m. this afternoon, June 28, 1993, at State Police Troop L Headquarters, East Farmingdale, N.Y.

By 9:00 A.M., the public information officer, Trooper Tom Collins, placed the press release on the fax machine in the communications division of headquarters, just off the lobby. He pressed the start button, instantly sending it to more than forty media agencies throughout the state. As the release slowly made its way through the machine, Collins braced himself for the flurry of phone calls he knew to expect. He'd been a public information liaison for more than eight years. He knew this was the type of story that would elicit a strong turnout at the news conference.

The fax marked the first time the media had heard of Joel Rifkin, but it didn't take long for them to react. By noon, an hour before the scheduled news conference, a large crowd of reporters and photographers gathered outside headquarters. But they would have to wait; the news conference would be delayed. Inside the small conference room, Capers and Louder weren't giving up. Their captain, Walter Heesch, urged them to press Rifkin harder. "This guy's too calm," he told the investigators. "Here's this body, it smells so awful, and he's riding around with it. And he's not excited; he's not upset. It's not like this is his first murder, where there were drugs and sex and he got excited and killed her. There have to be others. Start asking him if there are others."

They did.

"Is there anything more you want to tell us?" he asked casually.

Joel Rifkin said yes.

In the same matter-of-fact tone, Joel Rifkin began to tell the troopers how he'd strangled Jenny Soto. And Anna Lopez. He described how he'd killed Lorraine Orvieto and Mary-ann Hollomon. He spoke of the Hispanic woman, how he'd choked her to death and hidden her body under a mattress in an abandoned field near JFK Airport. The Korean one he'd murdered two years ago, stuffing her remains in a steamer trunk and throwing it into the Harlem river. Four of the women he strangled he'd jammed into fifty-five-gallon drums. He'd bought the drums in December of 1991. Within a few months, he told the investigators, he'd used them all.

Three women he'd dismembered, slinging their torsos and body parts into Manhattan rivers and canals. But mutilating bodies, he explained, got too bloody. And so he'd stopped.

A lot of corpses he'd just tossed into the woods—some in New York City, the East End of Long Island, even as far as upstate New York. Many times, Rifkin explained, he'd driven around a while, looking for the best locale.

Capers and Louder remained composed,

trying not to show their amazement. At first, they weren't sure if they even believed Joel Rifkin.

But the East Meadow landscaper was convincing. He told the investigators he began killing young women four years ago. His memory of some murders, Rifkin confessed, was murky. Others he recalled quite vividly. Overall, he felt pretty sure about the number: seventeen. Seventeen women—all young, and petite. All prostitutes, he said. He'd given them money; they'd given him sex.

Then he'd strangled them.

In a calm, almost disinterested manner, Joel Rifkin spoke of each of his macabre deeds, giving dates, descriptions, and locations. He tried to be helpful. He drew maps of areas where he'd stored bodies. He spelled names of some of his victims. Sometimes he only remembered a prostitute's street name, or what the woman had looked like. But he thought hard, trying to recall more.

Capers's mind was spinning. He had to make a choice: Should he try to draw Rifkin out slowly, case by case, or attempt to get as much as he could on every killing?

He opted for the latter approach. "What

about this one?" Capers kept repeating. "What happened to her?"

"I did her, too," Rifkin responded. "I strangled her."

Some of the killings, Rifkin bragged, had been easy. Others had not. Jenny Soto, he recalled, took a long time to die. He'd picked her up by the Williamsburg Bridge, off Houston Street in lower Manhattan. She was twenty-three years old.

"She fought the hardest," Rifkin said.

For the next four hours, as the media waited impatiently in the lobby, eager to learn more about the murder of Tiffany Bresciani, the detectives hunkered down with Rifkin, asking nonstop questions. Briefly, the cops considered setting up a video camera or getting a written confession, but they decided against it. Capers didn't want to risk doing anything that might trigger Joel Rifkin to stop talking.

So Joel Rifkin continued to talk. As the number of his victims escalated, Capers and Louder began to realize the enormity of what they faced. In a few hours they would break the news to the public. Within days, the story of Joel Rifkin and the women he had killed would spread from Long Island to headlines around the world. Law enforcement agencies all over New York State would face a voluminous task: to recover and identify almost two dozen bodies.

For the families of the victims, the news would be calamitous. It would devastate those who had already buried their loved ones—their daughters, sisters, in some cases, mothers—but hadn't known the circumstances behind their deaths.

And for those families who were missing someone, those who still had hope, it would be the end of a dream. For months, sometimes years, they had fought to stay optimistic: as long as there was no body, there was still a chance. But daily they battled their gut feelings—the ones that told them that something terrible, something deadly, had occurred.

Now, at last, they would have an answer: only not the one they'd prayed for.

For Jeanne Rifkin, the seventy-one-year-old white-haired mother at 1492 Garden Street, it would be a shocking discovery. It would prompt her to reflect on every moment of her son's upbringing—to ask the same question, over and over, the question that no one, except Joel Rifkin, could answer: Why did these women die?

Overnight, Jeanne Rifkin's son, the unemployed landscaper from East Meadow, would earn a new moniker: the Long Island serial killer.

Chapter 3

AS Capers and Louder interviewed Joel Rifkin, detectives fanned out along Garden Street in East Meadow.

Investigators Anthony Coppo and Kevin Walsh arrived first. They pulled up in front of 1492 Garden Street, on the corner of Spruce Lane, shortly after 6:00 A.M. Both men had been roused from bed two hours earlier and instructed to report to headquarters at once. After a briefing with senior investigators, they headed to East Meadow.

Their mission was simple: to learn more about the suspect. As they approached the Rifkin home, the cops couldn't help but notice how the gray-and-white wood raised ranch stood out. The front and side yards were made up of elaborate gardens surrounded by towering black oak trees. Among the medley of colorful flowers and plants were beds of lavender, lamb's ears, lilies, begonias, irises, and poppies. There was an ornate Japanese maple tree, a magnolia tree, and a black pine. The house, on a ninety-by-seventy-foot corner lot, looked tidy and inviting.

The investigators parked in front. For a while, they simply surveyed the area. Eventually Jan Rifkin emerged from the house, on her way to her job as a data processor. Around 8:00 A.M., not long after Jan's Toyota turned off Garden Street, the investigators knocked on the door of 1492.

Jeanne Rifkin peered through the small window. The investigators held up police badges. The seventy-one-year-old woman's heart began to race. Joel often stayed out late, but last night he hadn't come home at all. And now, police were on the porch.

Jeanne Rifkin quickly unlocked the door and pulled it open. She looked smaller than her five-foot-four-inch frame as she stood slightly hunched in the doorway.

"Can we come in?" Investigator Coppo asked.

Jeanne Rifkin nodded. She led the two men into the living room. The investigators got right to the point.

"Your son is at state trooper headquarters in Farmingdale," they told her. "He's being detained for a traffic violation."

"He's alright?" she asked, tense.

"He's fine."

Jeanne Rifkin breathed a sigh of relief. She thought for a moment. "What kind of violation?" she asked.

Now it was the cops' turn to pause.

"That's all the information we have," one of them told her.

For the next few minutes, Jeanne Rifkin answered questions. The investigators wanted to know if her son lived with her. She said he did. They asked what kind of car he drove. She told them about the Mazda pickups. He had two—one tan, the other gray. The investigators asked when she had last seen her son. She said the previous night. Joel, Jeanne Rifkin explained, had not come home. It wasn't like him, she added. It wasn't like him at all.

In a short time, several more police cars

pulled up in front of 1492 Garden Street. Some of the investigators began to canvass the neighborhood, knocking on doors up and down Garden Street and Spruce Lane. They asked each resident the same question: "How well do you know the Rifkins?"

Neighbors had little to say. The Rifkins were quiet, and kept to themselves, most explained. As for Joel, he was polite, but distant. He spent most days tinkering under his trucks or working in the garage. Sometimes he helped his mother with landscaping in the yard.

The Rifkins' next-door neighbors, Joy and Hal Reiter, knew the family best. Investigators quizzed them for a long time. They asked if they ever saw Joel with a woman. They wanted to know about his relationship with his family, or if he had any friends.

The Reiters said only good things about Joel Rifkin. They had always liked him.

"Joel is simply a gentle young man," Joy Reiter told the police.

The buzz along Garden Street spread like a brush fire. Something was going on. Something about Joel Rifkin. A neighbor called Joel's thirty-one-year-old sister, Jan, at work. The police, she explained, have been

around all day, asking about your brother.
What was going on?

Jan Rifkin had no idea. For the rest of the
afternoon she couldn't concentrate. She
stared at her computer, her mind turning
over possible scenarios. She called home repeatedly. There was no answer.

Throughout the day, Jeanne Rifkin tried to
query the investigators. What kind of traffic
violation? Why couldn't Joel call her? She
always got the same response: Her son was
being detained. That was all the information
they had.

A little past three, Jeanne Rifkin had had
enough. None of this made sense. She called
an attorney, a friend of the family who handled mostly civil cases. The elderly woman
explained what little she knew. She told the
lawyer the police had been around all day.

The family lawyer told her he suspected
Joel needed a criminal attorney. He suggested one—Robert Sale, fifty-six, a well-
known attorney from nearby Hempstead
who had handled several high-profile murder cases. One of Sale's associates was Eric
Naiburg, Amy Fisher's attorney.

The attorney offered to make the call for
her. It was 3:13 P.M. when Sale's secretary

buzzed him on an intercom. Sale put aside his legal briefs and picked up the phone.

The Rifkin family attorney explained the basics: A man named Joel Rifkin had been stopped by state troopers some twelve hours earlier for a traffic violation. He was still being held at police headquarters in East Farmingdale.

Sale was puzzled. He'd been a criminal attorney for more than thirty years. He knew the way the system worked. "How could that be?" he asked. "It sounds like something more substantial. Let me find out more."

Sale called Jeanne Rifkin. They spoke briefly. At Sale's request, she handed the phone to Investigator Walsh.

Sale got right to the point. "What's going on?" he asked.

"Counselor, we are preserving a crime scene," Walsh responded.

Sale pressed for details. "What exactly do you mean by a crime scene?" he said.

Walsh gave a vague answer, a general description of a crime scene. Sale began to get annoyed.

"Where is Mr. Rifkin?" he asked.

"He's being detained," Walsh said.

"Do you have a search warrant?"

The investigator admitted he did not.

"Look, unless you have a search warrant, I'm going to advise the Rifkins what their rights are," Sale said tersely. "What's the number of your headquarters?"

Walsh told him. Sale hung up and quickly dialed. He asked for Captain Walter Heesch.

"I'm sorry," the trooper on duty said. "Captain Heesch is in a meeting."

Sale then asked for Lieutenant Eugene Corcoran. He, too, was busy. The trooper took Sale's phone number.

"Someone will get back to you," he said.

Sale's temper blazed. A classic runaround, he thought. He wanted answers. Immediately. He tried again.

"I have a client, Joel Rifkin, I understand is there," Sale told the trooper firmly. "I insist on some information. Can you confirm he's there, and tell me why he's there and whether he's been arrested?"

"Someone," the trooper repeated, "will call you back."

"Okay," Sale said. "But unless someone calls me back in five minutes, I'm going to take appropriate action."

The attorney then dialed the Nassau County DA's office. Assistant District Attorney Fred Klein took the call. Klein had spent most of the day talking to senior investigators and studying police reports. In a short time, he planned to meet with a county court judge, to get a signature for a search warrant.

Klein ended the mystery.

"Your client is under arrest for a homicide," the prosecutor told Sale. "A body was found in his possession. He's being questioned in Farmingdale."

Sale quickly hung up the phone. Without a beat, he redialed headquarters. As the phone rang, the attorney pressed the tiny button on his talking watch. The watch had been a gift from his five sons. "It is four p-yem," it said.

At headquarters, the desk trooper on duty answered. Sale asked to speak with someone about the Rifkin case. In seconds, a familiar voice came on the line.

"Whom am I speaking with?" Sale asked.

"Lieutenant Corcoran," he was told.

Sale didn't hesitate. "What time do you have on your watch, Lieutenant? I'm calling at four P.M. Write down my name. I am Joel Rifkin's attorney and I'm directing there should be no further questioning of my client."

For a moment there was silence.

"I have four-oh-six P.M.," Lieutenant Corcoran said.

Sale lost his patience. "It's not," he snapped. "It's four-oh-two at the latest. In any event, I want you to stop questioning my client. I'm told you will comply with this."

Lieutenant Corcoran agreed. Almost at once, Capers and Louder ended their interrogation of Joel Rifkin. By now the detectives were exhausted. At that point, they had been grilling the East Meadow landscaper for some twelve hours. With the copious notes they had compiled, the detectives had plenty to keep them busy.

Outside state trooper headquarters, journalists were getting restless. The press conference had been postponed four times since the original time—1:00 P.M. To ease their wait, Trooper Collins shared a box of Dunkin Donuts one of the reporters had brought for him that morning, to celebrate Collins's twentieth anniversary on the job. The other journalists pounced, not leaving a crumb.

All afternoon, rumors had been circulating. There were more bodies. A lot more bodies. The number seventeen spread fast.

Trooper Collins sidestepped questions as best he could. He reminded journalists that he couldn't confirm anything—he didn't know the details himself. He encouraged the crowd to be patient. The story, he kept insisting, would be worth the wait.

It was. At 5:00 P.M., State Police Major Anthony DiResta, Jr., commander of State Police Troop L in East Farmingdale, and Captain Walter Heesch met with the press. DiResta read a prepared statement.

"All indications are that we have in custody a person who has committed multiple homicides," he said. "The degree of detail provided in the suspect's description gives us reason to believe this may be the largest case of serial murder since the Arthur Shawcross killings around Rochester in 1987 and 1989."

The reporters didn't need to be reminded about Shawcross. The Rochester man had been convicted of killing eleven prostitutes shortly after he arrived in that city in 1987. Previously, he had been paroled after serving 15 years for the 1972 murder of two children in Watertown, New York. During

his trial for the prostitution murders, Shawcross's attorneys argued that their client
was legally insane. The jury didn't buy it.
Shawcross was sentenced to a minimum of
250 years in jail.

DiResta described the arrest of Joel Rifkin,
how troopers had pursued the pickup and
eventually discovered the decomposing body.
He praised Capers and Louder. It was their
skill that had disarmed the suspect and encouraged him to detail his crimes. DiResta
reminded reporters that the investigation
was just beginning; even though police had
obtained a confession, no one knew for sure
if Joel Rifkin was indeed responsible for seventeen murders. The number could be
higher. It could be lower.

Questions flew. Reporters wanted details:
Who was the woman in the truck? Who were
the other sixteen? If everything Joel Rifkin
told detectives was true, how could so many
young women die and no one suspect a serial
killer was at large?

DiResta and Heesch offered little more. It
was much too early, they insisted, to get into
specifics. When pressed by reporters to characterize Joel Rifkin's demeanor, Captain
Heesch said that the landscaper had been

calm and composed. Despite his prodigious admission, Rifkin gave no motivation for his crimes. And he showed no remorse.

"If this is all true and he did commit these crimes, this is a very extraordinary case of human behavior," Heesch said.

The press conference was over. Journalists raced to East Meadow, eager to track down Rifkin's family members and friends. Meanwhile, investigators met to plan their next move: recovering and identifying bodies. Heesch was in charge. That night, the six-foot-eight-inch commander began delegating assignments. His boss, State Trooper Superintendent Thomas Constantine, summoned fifteen additional investigators from upstate divisions to work on the case. The detectives needed all the help they could get. The list of Joel Rifkin's victims was ominously long.

Chapter 4

ABOUT the time the story was unfolding in the press, Robert Sale broke the news to Jeanne and Jan Rifkin. He called them at home, shortly after ensuring the interrogation had ended. Sale knew there wasn't any easy way to tell the seventy-one-year-old and her daughter. But he didn't want the family to learn about Joel's arrest from the media. The attorney knew reporters would flock to the house immediately following the press conference.

Jan Rifkin had just returned from work. She pulled her Toyota to the curb a few hundred yards from the corner of Garden and Spruce. She couldn't get closer—police cars jammed the street, and about a dozen cops milled around. Panicky, Jan Rifkin ran into the house. Neighbors heard her hysterical sobs from a block away.

When he called, Sale could hear Jan Rifkin crying in the background. He spoke to Jeanne Rifkin. He asked her to be calm, and to sit down.

"I want to tell you something," he said gently. "This is not going to be pleasant. Joel is in custody. He's fine. But he has been arrested and charged with a homicide, in connection with a body allegedly found in the back of his truck. He is not coming home tonight. He is being held for court in the morning."

Sale paused. Jeanne Rifkin did not respond.

The attorney continued. "The police have said that Joel made a statement and as a result they are investigating other homicides. I have informed them that there will be no further questioning. I've requested that Joel be permitted to call you. In my opinion there might be a search warrant signed and the police might be searching the house later tonight. Don't disturb anything. If anybody arrives with a search warrant, call me at home. It will be read to me over the phone. And get a proper receipt."

Jeanne Rifkin could barely speak. She heard the attorney. She understood what he was saying. But she didn't believe him. She couldn't.

Sale asked Jeanne Rifkin to put one of the investigators on the phone. The attorney asked detectives to leave the house until they had a search warrant. The investigators complied. The screen door slammed as the men left the tidy living room of 1492 Garden Street, where they'd been waiting all day. Alone with her daughter, Jeanne Rifkin bent over in her chair. This couldn't be happening.

By now, a crowd had gathered outside 1492 Garden Street. Police cordoned off the street, and manned the sidewalk in front of the house. Dozens of photographers and camera operators milled around. Residents stood on their porch steps. Reporters perused the neighborhood, anxious to interview anyone who knew Joel Rifkin.

The Rifkins' next-door neighbors, Joy and Hal Reiter, spoke well of the family. They insisted Joel was a quiet, polite boy. Never any trouble. He and his sister were sweet, they said.

"I know it sounds like the kind of thing you always hear people say about someone who turns out to be a killer," Joy Reiter said. "But I can only say good things about Joel and his family. It's true."

But even the Reiters confessed that there were unanswered questions about Joel Rifkin.

"I guess none of us really knows what goes on behind closed doors," Joy Reiter said.

She glanced at the Rifkin house.

"I don't know how his mother will get through this," she said quietly.

As news of Rifkin's arrest traveled, former high school classmates began to show up in the neighborhood. Alan Whitlock, a thirty-four-year-old electrician, was among the first to arrive. He knew Joel from the high school photo club. He'd been to the Rifkin house several times. Reporters pounced, encircling him and firing questions.

Whitlock's mind was reeling. It was just by chance that he had been in the area when the news broke. That afternoon, he'd gone swimming in his mother-in-law's pool in East

Meadow, taking a break from the punishing heat. His wife, Sue, had waved from the porch.

"My sister just called," she called out. "She said they found a body on the corner of Spruce and Garden. Thousands of people are there. And news trucks."

Whitlock shrugged it off. But an hour later, when it was time to go home, he suggested they drive by the scene. It was only a few blocks out of the way.

As Whitlock neared, he noticed a childhood friend. He lowered the window.

"Hey, Al, didn't you go to school with that guy?" the friend asked.

"Who?"

"Joel Rifkin. He's the guy they arrested for murder."

"It can't be," Whitlock said slowly. "There must be two of them."

He turned to his wife. "I got to park the car," he said.

With daughter Lindsay, three, in his arms, Alan Whitlock rounded the corner of Spruce and Garden. His wife held Timmy, age one. The Whitlock's daughter Dawn, five, skipped on ahead.

Alan Whitlock couldn't believe it. "I knew

this guy," he kept repeating. "I used to hang out with him."

Sue Whitlock shivered. "Stop," she said. "You're scaring me."

Whitlock pointed to 1492 Garden Street. He remembered the fancy garden in front. "See the house—I've been in that house," he said.

Whitlock spotted another friend from high school. It was like old home week.

"Boy, this is something else, isn't it?" the friend said. "Pretty bizarre."

"Tell me about it," Whitlock replied. "You know, I used to hang out in this house."

The friend stopped. He stared. "You did?"

Before Whitlock could answer, the man began waving to reporters.

"Hey, over here," he shouted. "This guy was friends with Joel. He hung out with him. Hey, over here."

The red lights atop the camcorders went on. Microphones were thrust into Alan Whitlock's face.

"How do you feel about this?" he was asked.

"Are you surprised?"

"What do you remember about him from high school?"

For twenty minutes, Alan Whitlock thought hard, trying to remember more about Joel Rifkin. He told reporters what he recalled—that Joel was quiet, a loner who didn't have many friends. Whitlock insisted he couldn't believe that the guy he knew from high school was capable of murder.

When the cameras went off and most of the reporters went in search of others, two reporters stayed with Whitlock.

"One more question," a woman from the *New York Daily News* said. "Did Joel Rifkin ever mutilate animals?"

Whitlock laughed. "Are you talking about him or me?" he joked.

The reporter looked at him blankly. Whitlock decided it probably wasn't a good idea to joke around.

"Come on," he said, a bit annoyed. "How can you ask a question like that?"

"Well," the reporter said. "Lately there have been animal mutilations on Long Island."

Whitlock shrugged. As he turned to walk away, the other reporter, from the *New York Post,* grabbed his arm.

"Did you ever remember Joel having a social disease?" he asked.

Whitlock rolled his eyes. No, he didn't. He certainly didn't know Joel Rifkin that well.

"Look, that just wasn't talked about back then," he said. "I got to go."

And he did.

Youngsters on bicycles roamed around the neighborhood. "Serial killers don't live in East Meadow," one was heard to say. "This is wild."

Robyn Katz thought so too. The fifteen-year-old lived a few blocks away, on Lakeville Lane. On Monday night, not long after the news broke, she was on her way to hang out with friends at Prospect Park. She went the usual way, cutting through Garden Street.

Tonight, she could barely get through. She craned her neck to see what everyone was looking at. She squeezed past a few news trucks and sidled up to a state trooper.

"What happened?" she asked.

"Watch the news," the trooper answered, turning away. The cop was getting tired of answering the same question.

Katz tried again.

"Really," she said. "What's going on?"

The trooper barely looked at her. "He killed

prostitutes," he said, pointing to 1492 Garden Street. "A serial killer."

Katz hurried to the park. She shared the news with her friends. Later, she called her mother from a friend's house.

"Did you hear about the serial killer that lives in East Meadow?" she asked.

Her mother, Myra, had. "You may not walk home alone," she announced.

And Robyn didn't.

For the first time, Joel Rifkin faced a barrage of cameras as he was escorted from the front door of state trooper headquarters and taken back to Mineola, to Nassau County police headquarters. It was just before 9:30 P.M., roughly eighteen hours since Spaargaren and Ruane had signaled him to pull over on the parkway.

Before he left trooper headquarters, police confiscated Rifkin's clothing—the faded jeans, T-shirt, and red flannel shirt, even his shoes. The clothing was now considered evidence; police specialists would later examine it, looking for fibers, hair, and blood from Joel Rifkin's possible victims.

The cops provided Rifkin with a standard-issue white jumpsuit, complete with a hood and covers for his feet. Rifkin ducked his head slightly as the cameras began to flash. He did not respond as reporters shouted out questions.

"Did you do it, Joel?"

"Did you kill those women?"

Troopers drove Rifkin to Nassau County police headquarters in Mineola, just a few blocks from the spot where police had nabbed him earlier that day. He was led into a holding cell. To his dismay, police confiscated his glasses. Everything was blurred. Almost immediately Rifkin felt the onset of a migraine.

Joel Rifkin lay on a hard bunk that night, the day's events running through his mind. He must have known he would eventually get caught. He must have wondered why it took this long. For four years, he'd managed to keep his late-night carnage a secret. He'd fooled everyone: the cops, his family, even the young women who in desperation sold him their bodies. When they climbed into his car, they didn't know they would soon die. By the time they did, it was too late.

But now, as he lay awake in a holding cell, Joel Rifkin may have realized that it was over for him, too. Perhaps, at last, his deadly passion would be quelled. Forever.

As Joel Rifkin pondered his fate that night, more than a dozen detectives, armed with a search warrant, entered 1492 Garden Street. Earlier that day, investigators had met with Assistant District Attorney Fred Klein, giving him the necessary information to request a search warrant. Klein had brought the court order to County Court Judge Joanna Seybert. She'd reviewed it, asked a few questions, and signed it. By 8:00 P.M. the search warrant was ready. The DA's office delivered it to investigators.

The detectives displayed the search warrant to Jeanne Rifkin. She phoned Sale, and read it to him. The warrant permitted detectives to enter any room in the house—except for Jeanne and Jan Rifkin's bedrooms. They were also permitted access to the detached garage. Sale reminded Jeanne Rifkin to get a receipt from the police for whatever items they removed.

Investigators brushed past a silent Jeanne Rifkin and climbed the stairs to her son's second-floor bedroom. They pushed open the

door and entered the private world of Joel
Rifkin.

What they encountered rendered them
speechless.

Chapter 5

AS more than a dozen detectives rifled through her home, Jeanne Rifkin sequestered herself in her bedroom on the first floor, just off the kitchen. She tried to block out the horror of the past twelve hours. She couldn't sleep. She'd barely eaten all day. In the next room, her daughter was inconsolable.

The phone rang continuously. Jeanne told Jan not to answer it. The seventy-one-year-old woman got adept, fast, at turning down interviews. When *Newsday* phoned, shortly after police announced the arrest, Jeanne Rifkin cut off the caller midsentence.

"I'm sorry," she said crisply. "I have no comment."

As the days passed, Jeanne Rifkin found herself looking back on her life. Losing her husband six years earlier had been excruciating. It didn't compare to the pain she felt now.

She attempted to piece together what had gone wrong. She had tried to be a good mother—that she knew. Her husband, Ben, had been devoted to Joel and to Jan as well.

Jeanne Rifkin remembered the early days. From the beginning of her marriage, she and her husband had wanted a child. For a long time, it seemed as if it wouldn't happen.

Then there was Joel. They adopted him in the winter of 1959, three weeks after he was born to two unwed students. Back then, the Rifkins lived in a small ranch house in New City in upstate New York. Baby Joel was a blessing, the miracle that the couple had prayed for. When he came into their lives, Ben was forty; Jeanne thirty-seven.

When Joel was a toddler they were blessed again. In 1962 they adopted Jan.

The adoptions were never a secret; both children knew that Jeanne and Ben were not their biological parents. But the Rifkins always reminded their kids that they were special—and very much wanted.

In 1965, when Joel was six and Jan three, the Rifkins moved to Garden Street in East Meadow. They enrolled Joel in Prospect Avenue Elementary School down the block, adjacent to a large playground.

Ben Rifkin took a job as a structural engineer at Brookhaven National Laboratory in Stony Brook. Jeanne took care of the house, and when the children were older, she worked part-time as a recreational therapist. For many years, Jeanne's father lived with the family. There was always someone home when Joel and Jan returned from school.

Almost daily, Jeanne Rifkin worked in the garden. As he grew older, Joel began to take an interest in horticulture too. Joel mowed the lawn and helped his mother trim hedges and plant trees. As they worked together, Jeanne Rifkin taught her son about foliage.

Mother and son shared other interests as well. Both loved photography. Jeanne Rifkin was skilled at needlepoint, lapidary, and jewelry making. Joel enjoyed crafts too. He worked with driftwood, and in high school he did silk-screening on T-shirts for a neighbor who played in the orchestra. On the T-shirts he printed VIOLA POWER.

Jeanne Rifkin had another passion: education. She and her husband were committed to improving the school system for their children. When Joel was in the fifth grade, Ben Rifkin was elected to the East Meadow School Board for a three-year term. At a reorganization meeting midway through his tenure, Ben Rifkin was appointed vice-president by fellow board members.

When school board elections neared, Jeanne Rifkin spent hours on the telephone, calling neighbors and encouraging them to vote. Ben canvassed the neighborhood on foot, knocking on doors and handing out leaflets about the candidates.

Ben Rifkin also joined the board of trustees of the East Meadow Public Library. Between his responsibilities on the school board and the library, Ben Rifkin spent several nights a week at meetings. For many years, Joel worked at the library after school. He was a page, sorting and arranging books on the shelves.

Although he was bright (his IQ was tested at 128), Joel did poorly in school. In lower grades, Joel often got 30s and 50s on relatively easy tests and had difficulty learning to read. Years later, the family learned he had dyslexia. Back then, they knew only that school was difficult for Joel. Almost every evening Jeanne spent hours tutoring her son, reviewing homework and listening patiently as he painstakingly read aloud.

Because of his work on the school board, Ben Rifkin got to know most of his son's teachers. It put added pressure on Joel. Although his marks improved somewhat in high school—he graduated with about an 80 average—Joel's middling grades were a disappointment to the family. And Joel knew it.

Throughout his school years, Joel Rifkin also had a tough time fitting in with his peers. Other children made fun of him. In elementary school, they nicknamed him the Turtle, because of his stooped shoulders and slow gait. Later, in high school, his socialization problems would grow worse. After Rifkin's arrest, one former childhood classmate seemed to sum up the sentiment; he recalled a time when he'd glimpsed Joel's latest failing test grade and remarked to a friend, "The Turtle is such a loser."

* * *

In other ways, Joel Rifkin had a seemingly normal upbringing. The Rifkin family spent time together. In the summers, they had barbecues in the yard, took day trips to the beach, and went on vacation in the Catskill Mountains in upstate New York, staying in roadside motels. Now and then, Ben and Joel went off fishing alone. Joel treasured those outings with his dad.

Joel and Jan fought like typical siblings. Some of their battles centered on use of the upstairs bathroom, which they shared. They had their own bedrooms, and their own pets. Joel kept a turtle and a snake in a cage. Jan had a Siamese cat named Hector who was declawed in order to keep him from ruining the furniture. Several times a day, Jan attached a leash to the cat's collar and took Hector for a stroll in the neighborhood.

Although they were Jewish, the Rifkins did not attend synagogue. Unlike many of the Jewish children in the neighborhood, Joel and Jan did not join the youth group at Temple Emanuel or at the East Meadow Jewish Center, a few blocks from their home. When he reached adolescence, Joel did not have a bar mitzvah.

Ben and Jeanne Rifkin had a strong marriage. They often took walks together in the neighborhood, holding hands. Ben was proud of Jeanne's talent in landscaping and other creative arts. Once the children were grown, and Jeanne's father had passed away, the couple managed to get away alone together a few times. On several occasions, they traveled to Europe.

Ben Rifkin was an outgoing, affable man. He was well liked in the neighborhood, and in his community. When he died, members of the board of trustees at the library voted to name a wing of the branch in his memory.

He was remembered as a progressive man. In the early 1970s he joined a men's group whose members met every week to discuss ways to improve their relationships with women, and to understand their changing role in society.

On the board of education, Ben Rifkin advocated students' rights and encouraged young people to get involved in the political process.

"He was ahead of his time," recalled Superintendent Frank Saracino, who served as principal of the East Meadow High School from 1976 to 1988. "If someone was trying to be harsh on a student, Ben would always be there to remind them to recognize the student as a human being, someone who should be treated with dignity. He was not the type to come down hard on someone because they were subservient to him."

On the board, Ben Rifkin always managed to get his point across without pushing too hard. "He believed in the dignity of the person," Saracino recalled. "He wasn't given to being boisterous or heated."

Shortly after his father's term on the school board ended, Joel Rifkin graduated from Woodland Junior High School and moved on to East Meadow High School.

Once again, Joel Rifkin tried to fit in. Once again, he was rebuffed. His classmates thought he was strange; he wore wire-rimmed glasses and dressed oddly—his pants were too short, his white socks always showed. When he asked girls for dates, they turned him down. Many times he ate lunch alone.

Other students teased him. They called him a host of degrading names. His childhood moniker, Turtle, followed him throughout his schooling. In high school, however, more degrading nicknames emerged—nerd, doofus, oddball, creep, jerk. And worse.

After Rifkin's arrest, former classmates admitted with some embarrassment that they'd given Joel Rifkin a hard time over the years. One man confessed he regularly yelled, "Hey, asshole, get out of my way," whenever he encountered Rifkin in the halls. When they met, Joel would immediately retreat; he'd duck his head, mumble, and walk away.

The former classmate said he and a friend used to grab Joel and play catch with him, occasionally throwing him into the lockers. "I'd push him, he'd fall down," the man recalled. "I'm not proud of this by any means, but, you know, you got the order of life—jocks, class A's, freaks, burnouts. Joel was on the bottom. He was an abuse unit. He was subtly obnoxious, like, his presence annoyed you. I remember really ticking him off, and he never took a swing. I guess we were trying to get a rise out of him because he was so strange. I could see him get so enraged that he'd be shaking. He would just stand there. He almost seemed like he wanted it."

Only once did Joel Rifkin fight back. It was in his junior year. He saw a classmate, also an outcast, taking a beating in the school-yard. Joel jumped in and starting swinging. With a strength no one knew he had, Rifkin yanked the teenagers apart roughly and stood in the middle, shaking with anger. The look on his face frightened both boys.

In an attempt to fit in somewhere, Joel Rifkin participated in a variety of extracur-ricular activities. In freshman year, he joined the cross-country track team. He wasn't the slowest runner on the team, yet his teammates dubbed him Lard-ass. At prac-tice, Rifkin trained alone. When the others circled the track together, he headed outside the gates and ran around the school grounds.

Over the next three years, Rifkin's team-mates tormented him. They hid his running gear and planted phony letters in his lock-ers, supposedly from girls who wanted to date him. One Friday night in his junior year, four track members, drunk on beer, surrounded each exit of the East Meadow Library, where Rifkin was working after school. Every time he tried to get out, they pelted him with eggs.

Finally, Rifkin called his father. The boys ran off as Ben Rifkin's car approached.

It was in the school's basement lockers, however, that Joel Rifkin took the most abuse. Every afternoon after practice, members of the track team as well as those on the football and lacrosse teams harassed Rifkin. There was no escape. They sprayed him in the showers, stole his towel, and held his head under running water.

After Rifkin's arrest, former classmates studied the yearbook picture of the cross-country team. Everyone in the photo wore the regulation blue East Meadow High School sweatshirt—except Joel Rifkin.

"I don't remember why, but I would guess maybe he didn't have his sweatshirt because probably one of us threw it in the shower," said Mark Vangasteren, one of the other runners on the team. "It was the kind of thing we did to him all the time. We were cruel to him. In high school, there are the picked on and those who do the picking on, and I happened to be a picker-on. I feel bad about that now."

Some of the aspersions were more subtle. Once, the cross-country team participated in a week-long preseason training camp near New London, Connecticut. The camp was attended by high school runners from throughout Long Island.

To get there, Joel hitched a ride with another teammate. But when it was time to go home, the teammate left without him. No one else offered Joel a ride home. He stood outside, silently, as everyone else loaded their bags into cars and drove off. When the last car disappeared from sight, Joel called his father. Ben Rifkin drove more than three hours to pick up his son.

Vangasteren remembered that day. "My parents came to pick me up and I could have offered him a ride," he said. "But I didn't. I herded my parents out right away, because I didn't want him catching a ride with me. It was like that. It was nothing he did. It was just you didn't want to be around him."

Word of the incident spread in school over the next few days. Many students laughed at the image of Joel Rifkin left alone by the side of the road. But Alan Whitlock, who knew Joel from the photo club, recalled how he and several of his friends had felt badly for Rifkin. "We couldn't believe the team had done that to him," he said. "It was so mean."

Yet despite the abuse, Rifkin tried to befriend his tormentors. He often invited his teammates to his house when his parents were away. Sometimes, they accepted the invitation. "We would go over and have the run of the place," said Vangasteren. "Watch TV, drink beer, do whatever we wanted. We used him, to be blunt about it. He was easy to make fun of. He would usually laugh, even if we were being really cruel. He didn't show any sign of feeling the pain. It's not something I'm proud of, but that's how it was."

In the beginning of his senior year, Joel quit the track team. By then, he'd achieved his goal: he'd earned a varsity letter. Even that was a hollow victory. To earn a letter, a runner had to score at least one point in a varsity track meet. At the last meet of the year, Rifkin's coach let everyone who hadn't gotten a letter participate, just to earn the letter.

Rifkin joined the debating team, the yearbook staff, and the photo club. He also spent a lot of time with the AV crew, setting up microphones and projectors for slide shows.

But Joel didn't fare much better in those cliques. One afternoon while he was working in the darkroom, fellow photo staffers stole his camera. When he emerged and asked for

it, the boys, straight-faced, claimed igno-
rance.

Joel never mentioned it again. Eventually,
he got a new camera.

Some insist that there were others at East
Meadow High School who shouldered far
more ridicule than Joel Rifkin. One over-
weight student, in fact, had a particularly
difficult time.

"He was picked on far more than Joel Rifkin," said Ben Mevorach, who attended East
Meadow High School and is now news director for WGSM, a Long Island radio station.
"We had others that had other quirks. Joel
wasn't the only one who got a hard time."

If ever there was a place where Joel Rifkin
did not get teased, it was probably at the
school newspaper, the *Jet Gazette*. He took
pictures and did some writing. The biggest
perk to working on the newspaper, however,
was having a place to hang out in between
classes.

That was Joel's favorite part, too. He
headed to the office, on the first floor around
the corner from the cafeteria, as often as he
could. He didn't mind when it was his turn
to sell pretzels—fifty cents apiece—to help

raise funds. For Joel Rifkin it was a rare opportunity to socialize.

During senior year, Joel's parents gave him a dark blue two-door Toyota to drive the two miles to and from school. On several occasions, Rifkin offered Alan Whitlock a ride home. Sometimes the teenagers stopped at a record store and browsed. Now and then they dropped by the Rifkin house and hung out in Joel's room, listening to rock music. Joel had a good-quality stereo system with a built-in tape deck. He liked to crank up the volume when playing his favorite tunes—the Eagles' "Hotel California" and Led Zeppelin's "Stairway to Heaven." On the walls of his bedroom were photos he had taken—mostly black-and-white shots of scenery or crowds.

Looking back, Alan Whitlock insists that nothing about Joel's life or his behavior seemed unusual. "He'd snap at his sister when she knocked on the door—'Leave us alone'—and give one-word answers—'Fine'—when his mother asked how his day had gone." Whitlock said. "That's the way all teenagers are."

But Whitlock recalled that Joel Rifkin never talked about girls. Or his family. "He never said much about anything," he said.

"Never talked about any girls in school. Didn't mention his family. Once I said something like, 'Your mom is so nice. You don't look like her, though.' And he said, 'My sister and I are adopted.' And that was it. He didn't want to talk about it anymore."

In many ways, Joel Rifkin's family life remains shrouded in mystery. By all accounts, Ben and Jeanne Rifkin were nurturing and concerned parents. Ben Rifkin attended all of his son's track meets, cheering from the bleachers. Jeanne Rifkin shared her love of nature with her oldest child.

But Joel Rifkin's ambitious and tenacious parents may have proved daunting role models. Clearly, Joel Rifkin grew up with none of their energy and self-confidence.

Instead, he retreated. He learned to dismiss the abandonment and ridicule he suffered in school. He skillfully internalized his anger. But something ominous was developing in his mind.

Experts suggest that a serial killer harvests violent sexual fantasies for ten to fifteen years before he acts on them. It is likely, then, that the early stages of Joel Rifkin's monstrous intents hatched during his troubled high school years.

Did he try to fight them? Did he know his desires were lurid, his reverie appalling? When did the seeds of his odious plan to kill prostitutes first develop?

There is no way to know.

"I keep looking back in disbelief," says Superintendent Saracino. "The kind of kid he was—maybe forty, fifty kids a year fit the same profile. He just blended into the woodwork. You'd never notice him."

Perhaps that was the problem. Maybe Joel Rifkin wanted to be noticed; to make his mark. One thing is clear. It was at age eighteen, a graduating senior at East Meadow High School, that Joel Rifkin began to patronize prostitutes. Was he seeking acceptance? Or revenge?

It was a deadly beginning.

Chapter 6

BY the time he graduated from East Meadow High School in 1977, Joel Rifkin had goals—but little motivation to achieve them. At his parents' urging, he applied to the State University at Brockport in upstate New York.

Rifkin had trouble staying focused. For the next decade his education was a series of stops and starts. He attended the Brockport school for two years, taking various liberal arts courses and living off campus in a town house complex. In the spring of 1980 he dropped out. He moved back to his parents' home in East Meadow and enrolled at a nearby school, Nassau Community College.

He took a range of courses over the next few years, but usually quit midsemester. By 1984 he'd earned only twelve credits.

His social life was practically nonexistent. Back in Brockport he'd had his first—and likely his only—girlfriend. For a year, he dated a heavyset woman he met on campus. The ex-girlfriend described him as "sweet, but always depressed." During their relationship he cut classes and began to neglect his appearance. "He didn't work hard at all," she said. "I knew his parents were upset. He told me they were going to be very disappointed."

In between attempts at his halfhearted academic career, Joel Rifkin worked at various jobs on Long Island, seldom earning above minimum wage. For a while he worked in sales at a Record World in the Roosevelt Field Mall in Hempstead. It seemed like a good job for him. As a teenager Joel Rifkin had spent many hours in that store, reading album covers and listening to piped-in tunes. He knew a lot about the latest bands.

But he had trouble keeping up with the pace. He easily fell behind in his work. And as it had been in other areas of his life, Joel Rifkin didn't fit in with his peers. While other employees hung out together after work, Joel Rifkin kept to himself. Sometimes, at the start of his shift, he barely greeted coworkers.

Shortly after Rifkin's arrest, a former manager from Record World called in to a New York radio station. Joel Rifkin, the man insisted, was one strange guy.

"He was a total piece of work," he said. "This guy couldn't even count to ten. Every time we tried to do deposits at the end of the day he would always foul up. He couldn't get it right. He used to come in, dirt under his nails, oil or grease, God knows what else."

Rifkin quit Record World after about a year. He took a part-time job as a salesman in a children's store, Coronet Juvenile in Westbury. By now he was twenty-five years old and—except for his brief stint at Brockport—had never lived on his own. In the summer of 1984 Joel Rifkin rented a cramped studio on the second floor of a private house in Levittown. But in a short time he quit his job. It wasn't long before he had trouble paying the rent. Joel Rifkin returned to 1492 Garden Street.

Over the next couple of years Rifkin drifted in and out of jobs. But he harbored a dream: he wanted to be a writer, a great one. He spent hours alone in his bedroom reading literary masters and struggling to compose his own poetry. Seldom was he satisfied with his work.

Jeanne Rifkin knew about her son's passion for writing, and his aspiration for fame. At times, it worried her. Once she shared her concerns with her next-door neighbor, Joy Reiter. "You know, Joel has dreams," she said almost sadly. "And I hope he will achieve them."

Rifkin continued to dabble in photography. Once, on an outing with his parents to the Metropolitan Museum of Art in Manhattan, he brought along his camera and shot portraits of Ben and Jeanne in the Egyptian wing, before the Temple of Dendur.

Sometimes Rifkin took his camera to the beach. He snapped photos of the pier or a distant boat on the horizon. He experimented, capturing the same image over and over, varying the exposure slightly each time. His precision was an aberration: everything else in his life, it seemed, was aimless and chaotic.

His homelife had begun to unravel, too. In

the fall of 1986, Ben Rifkin fell ill. Doctors gave a grim diagnosis: prostate cancer.

Ben Rifkin tried to make things easier for his wife and children. He kept his spirits up, and seldom complained, even when the pain was intense. But on February 20, 1987, a few weeks after his sixty-eighth birthday, Ben Rifkin could no longer endure the pain.

He took an overdose and wrote a note to his family: "Dearest Jeanne, Jan, and Joel, Please forgive me for committing suicide . . ."

At the funeral, Joel Rifkin, then twenty-eight, gave a eulogy. His words brought mourners to tears. The young man told the crowd that he was adopted, but that it hadn't mattered in his family. His father, Joel said, was a special man.

"He did not give me life, he gave me love," Joel said.

Although they were not religious, the Rifkin family sat *shivah* for the next week—the traditional Jewish mourning period. Neighbors brought plates of food, and friends dropped by. Those who loved Ben Rifkin shared their memories of him.

Soon after Ben Rifkin's death, members of the library board agreed that he deserved a

special remembrance for his years of service
and devotion: that year, they named a wing
of the branch in his honor.

In many ways, the suicide of his father
caused Joel Rifkin to sink even deeper into
the portentous and disturbing world he had
created. As he had for years, Joel Rifkin
continued to solicit sex from prostitutes.
Late at night, he cruised the streets of Hempstead and lower Manhattan. Always, he was
selective; he hunted for a long time before he
chose a woman.

For some time, the fantasies must have
been growing. Each time he had sex with a
prostitute Joel Rifkin fought a troubling,
rabid desire. His frustration and fury
swelled.

Something would push him over the edge.

Some wonder if it was his relationship with
Kathryn Mary Kelty. He met her a few weeks
after his father's death, when he stopped in
a pizzeria on Bell Boulevard, in Bayside,
Queens. Kelty, a waitress, was seated at a
table, scribbling in a notebook. The two
struck up a conversation. Kelty explained
that she was working on a screenplay. Rif-

kin told her that he, too, was a screenwriter. He'd just completed a short story entitled "The Frosh," about a student's antics at college. Then he lied, telling Kelty he was a student at New York University.

Kelty, a divorced mother of two, was impressed. She and Rifkin exchanged phone numbers. Over the next few months they talked frequently about Kelty's screenplay. Kelty liked to brag that she was an accomplished writer. She read a few of Rifkin's works, and told him that he, too, had enormous talent. For perhaps the first time, Joel Rifkin felt important. Someone actually liked him—an attractive young woman who not only listened to his dreams but shared them as well.

Rifkin quickly became enamored of the sprightly blond. He began to hope their friendship would grow into something more.

In the summer of 1987 Kelty rented a one-bedroom apartment on Forty-ninth Street in Manhattan and invited Rifkin to move in, sharing the living room with another male roommate. Kelty outlined the conditions: he would pay rent, help keep the apartment neat, and most importantly, edit her screenplay.

Joel Rifkin agreed instantly. His mother was unhappy. It was just a few months after her husband's death and Jeanne Rifkin was lonely. Besides, she was worried about Joel. She'd met Kathryn Kelty once, when Joel had brought her home. Jeanne Rifkin didn't like her.

But Joel Rifkin was resolute; he packed a few things and left.

For a short time, the Manhattan arrangement worked nicely. To Rifkin's disappointment, however, his relationship with Kelty remained platonic. Several times he attempted to kiss her but she always brushed him off.

At night, Rifkin joined her at after-hours bars and clubs. They went to Xenon and Area—all the fashionable spots in town. He passed up offers for drugs and didn't drink. Every night was the same; as Kelty danced unrestrained for hours, Rifkin roamed the edge of the bar, silently watching the young woman move.

When the pair left the clubs it was usually near dawn. Joel Rifkin always eyed the prostitutes traipsing along Ninth Avenue. His fascination for the girls of the street never diminished.

After six weeks, Kelty and Rifkin had a falling-out. He hadn't worked at all on her screenplay, and she was getting tired of his excuses. Then Rifkin took a job at a courier service. Kelty was indignant. Now, she figured, he'd never start editing.

In a heated argument, Kelty pulled out a knife and threw Rifkin out of the apartment. "Pack your things and get out," she screamed. Years later, she explained it to detectives.

"I just couldn't stand him anymore," she said.

It is unclear if Rifkin knew at that time how Kathryn Mary Kelty made her living. Now, Kelty will only say that she is "retired" and has AIDS. But police believe she had worked the streets.

One thing Kelty wants made clear: she was never Joel Rifkin's girlfriend. When her name and picture emerged following Rifkin's arrest, some of the media reported she was. "I never fucked him," she told reporters. "But this creep was crazy about me. I'm lucky to be alive."

The experience with Kelty unsettled Rifkin. He felt rejected and bitter. Once again he moved back to his second-floor bedroom at 1492 Garden Street. All of the plans he'd made with the young woman—the vision of being famous writers—were destroyed. Joel Rifkin had yet again failed to make his mark.

At home, the mood was somber. In the months following her husband's death, Jeanne Rifkin had become withdrawn. She didn't return friends' phone calls and seemed to lose interest in everything. She dropped weight and stopped coloring her hair. Overnight, it seemed, her dark curls turned to gray and then to white. Suddenly, Jeanne Rifkin looked old.

Neighbors tried to help. Joy Reiter called out to Jeanne that summer after Ben's death, when she and her husband, Hal, were relaxing on lounge chairs in their yard.

"Jeanne, come sit with us," Joy said kindly.

Jeanne Rifkin did. Through her tears, she told her old friends how unhappy she was. She broke down crying. "I miss Ben so much," she kept saying.

Over time, Jeanne Rifkin tried to channel her energy back into the projects she'd always enjoyed. She continued working in the garden. By then she'd expanded it—she planted flowers and bushes along a small strip next to the garage, an area that had previously been a patch of grass. Occasionally, Joel helped his mother move heavy bushes.

That summer, Joel Rifkin may have tried to turn his life around. He announced plans to open a landscaping business. He also decided to go back to school, this time to study horiticulture. Jeanne Rifkin was pleased. Her son finally appeared to have a clear vision for the future. Joel Rifkin bought a 1978 Chevy van to use for the business, and applied to the agricultural program at the State University of New York at Farmingdale.

But Joel Rifkin's hidden longings continued to disrupt his world. A few weeks after he moved back to East Meadow, Rifkin was arrested by Hempstead Village cops for offering a prostitute twenty dollars for oral sex. It was shortly after midnight on August 22, 1987. Rifkin posted the $75 bail himself, but ignored a court appearance a few months later. Eventually, he paid a $250 fine.

Rifkin did not say a word about the incident to anyone. He was grateful his mother didn't know. She was suffering enough.

In the fall, a few weeks after his arrest, Rifkin enrolled in the two-year agricultural college at the State University at Farmingale. He did well in his classes in ornamental horiticulture. After his first year, he applied for an internship at Planting Fields Arboretum in Upper Brookville. Plantings Fields is a 409-acre public garden on the North Shore of Long Island. It has approximately 160 acres of gardens and plant collections, 40 acres of lawns, and 200 acres of fields and woodlands.

To be considered for the internship, Joel Rifkin wrote an essay explaining why he wanted to be a horticulturist. Then, he was interviewed by the assistant director. He was one of a handful who were accepted.

It was quite an achievement. Jeanne Rifkin was delighted. Joel Rifkin was assigned to the grounds crew—planting and watering, and mowing lawns. He made slightly more than minimum wage, and worked there for almost ten months.

But again Joel Rifkin had trouble connecting with others. His employers didn't feel he showed the same enthusiasm and love of nature as the other interns. Within weeks, Rifkin drifted off on his own, barely speaking to anyone.

Rifkin became widely known at the arboretum for his strange designs. Shortly after he began working on the grounds he planted annuals in one of the specialty gardens. It was an area on the north border of the park reserved for dwarf conifers—naturally occurring pine trees. When the annuals blossomed, jokes were traded throughout the arboretum.

"It's so inappropriate," longtime horticulturist Bill Barish used to think when he saw the flowers sprinkled among the diminutive pine trees. "How silly it looks."

Barish wasn't surprised to hear from his colleagues that it had been the intern, Joel Rifkin, who planted the annuals. "He might have studied horticulture, but his ideas are a little off the wall," Barish said, shaking his head.

In the spring of 1989, almost at the end of the SUNY agricultural program, Joel Rifkin's grades plummeted and he dropped out. By then, his internship at Planting Fields had ended.

It was April of 1989. Rifkin decided to concentrate on his landscaping business. He registered a trailer and hooked it to his green Chevy van.

He got a few jobs right away: SUNY Farmingdale and Planting Fields, after all, were solid credentials.

One of his first tasks was to take care of the grounds of the Casey estate in Rosyln Harbor, Long Island. William Casey, the former director of the CIA, had died two years before. His widow, Sophia, called Planting Fields, looking for a gardener. Someone suggested Joel Rifkin.

Sophia Casey explained her needs; she wanted Rifkin to dig up a troublesome patch of grass in the yard and replace it. The area was zoysia, a perennial with fine wiry leaves. She wanted it replaced because it didn't turn green as early as the rest of the lawn. She told Rifkin she would pay him eight dollars an hour. She expected him to work every day.

He didn't. For the next two months Rifkin worked sporadically, and never seemed to accomplish much. Then one day he left and never returned.

* * *

Joel Rifkin's world had begun a faster downhill spiral. His business was a failure. He'd never completed his schooling. He got into several car accidents and was ticketed for speeding. Rifkin never paid fines, so his license was suspended and his registration revoked. He began to dress slovenly. After working on lawns or tinkering underneath his trucks all day, Rifkin seldom cleaned up. With grease and dirt under his nails, his appearance deteriorated.

Even some of the prostitutes in New York City say they turned him down. There was something unappealing about Joel Rifkin. Something odd. Always, it seemed, he looked as if he had a secret. An eerie secret.

Indeed he did. His fantasy world was on the fringe of becoming reality. The almost painful urges he must have been fighting since adolescence grew too powerful. The visions consumed him.

By then, Rifkin had stopped soliciting hookers on Long Island; the arrest in Hempstead had scared him. Instead, he'd begun to travel into Manhattan, cruising the Lower East Side off Allen Street, and Twelfth Street and Second Ave.

It was time. Joel Rifkin was about to make

his mark. No longer would he feel inadequate. Women like Kathryn Mary Kelty could never reject him again.

Now, he even had role models. In recent months, Rifkin had begun to follow the trial of Arthur Shawcross, the Rochester man accused and eventually convicted of killing eleven prostitutes. Rifkin carefully clipped out newspaper articles about the killings. He was keeping a scrapbook.

He also studied the case of an unknown serial killer, who police believe was responsible for the murders of forty-nine women in the Seattle area. Rifkin even read a book on the subject: *The Search for the Green River Killer.*

Both serial killers picked up prostitutes, had sex with them, and then murdered them. In most instances, they tied up their victims. They enjoyed watching the terrified young women scream for their lives, begging for mercy.

Perhaps Joel Rifkin thought he would too.

Chapter 7

AS police hunted through Joel Rifkin's bedroom the night of the arrest, they uncovered the Shawcross clippings and the book on the Green River killings. But strewn about the room were even more grisly findings.

Detectives discovered dozens of "trophies"—mementos taken from Rifkin's victims. On the floor, in desk drawers, even posted to the wall were dozens of ID cards, driver's licenses, library cards, credit cards, and photographs. Jenny Soto's wallet was there, and Mary Ellen DeLuca's driver's license. They found one of Anna Lopez's earrings.

There were piles of women's clothing—panties, bras, sweaters, stockings. In a blue metal safe were dozens of earrings and necklaces, gold bracelets and rings. Scattered throughout the room were several makeup cases, pocketbooks, even a hair curler. Police gathered it all, placing the evidence in plastic bags.

In the garage, investigators immediately detected a putrid smell. It came from an orange wheelbarrow. Cops drew three ounces of blood from the inside. They found a pair of women's panties on the floor, as well as a stockpile of rope and tarp. On a gas chain saw they made yet another grim discovery: bloodstains and bits of human flesh.

When questioned later, neighbors admitted that they had smelled foul odors emanating from the Rifkin garage for some time. They said they thought it was from pesticides Joel and his mother used in the garden.

In all, the detectives' search took six hours. At one point, a trooper made a run to the local pizzeria, Tucci's, in town. He brought back ten pies with assorted toppings. The investigators stopped their dismal task to eat.

When they were done with their search,

police had removed 228 items. They took 115 from the upstairs bedroom, 91 from the garage, 21 from the basement, and 1 item from another small room upstairs.

When told about the trophies, Jeanne Rifkin confessed softly that she knew nothing about it—she never ventured into her son's room. Investigators felt sorry for the diminutive widow, clearly in shock. But they could barely conceal their amazement. How much had she overlooked in her son's deadly past?

In all, police found names of ten women in Joel Rifkin's room. In some cases, the names helped cops link long-unidentified bodies to Rifkin. In other cases, the serial killer himself offered names of the women he had strangled.

The bodies of most of Rifkin's victims had already been found. Some had been identified through fingerprints and dental records. Some lay in Potter's Field, the dumping ground for unclaimed corpses. Rifkin's confession helped police find two more bodies.

Back at state trooper headquarters, Captain Walter Heesch grew even more determined; every one of Joel Rifkin's victims would be found and identified. In life, they'd been cheated. In death, they deserved the dignity of a name on their grave.

Within a few days of the arrest, Heesch announced that state police had linked eighteen murders to Joel Rifkin, one more than Rifkin had admitted to Capers and Louder. By the summer of 1993, police had identified eleven. They were still searching for four bodies; they were still trying to identify three they had.

All of the women were petite—under five foot three, and weighing around a hundred pounds. Joel Rifkin said they were all prostitutes; police believe they probably were.

Almost all the women were picked up on the streets of Manhattan, mostly from the Lower East Side. They almost all suffered from drug addictions.

Joel Rifkin smothered or strangled them, sometimes during sex or immediately afterwards. He took a memento from each—unfastening an earring, removing panties, pocketing credit cards. He stored the bodies for days in various locations. Then he disposed of them in diverse ways.

"He went, picked up a prostitute, had sex

with her, killed her, and dumped her," said Heesch.

Tragically, it was that simple.

The first two women to die at the hands of Joel Rifkin have never been found. He strangled them and cut their bodies into pieces. He told police it was easier to transport them that way. He murdered the first in 1989, the second in 1990. He told police he didn't remember exactly where he'd disposed of the body parts. He thought he had dumped one into a canal in New York City and the other in waters off New Jersey.

Rifkin took a breather for a while. Then in the spring of 1991 he met Barbara Jacobs.

Jacobs lived on the Lower East Side. In 1979 she had been arrested for car theft. Since then, Jacobs had been in and out of jails in drug and prostitution cases. She was small—five-three and around a hundred pounds. Her decomposed nude body was found wrapped in a plastic garbage bag inside a cardboard box on July 14, 1991, in the Hudson River off Pier 95. It was eleven days before her thirty-second birthday.

For two years, her death was listed incorrectly. A medical examiner had ruled that

Jacobs died of acute cocaine intoxication. She didn't. Barbara Jacobs was strangled.

So was Yun Lee. The body of the thirty-one-year-old Korean prostitute was discovered on September 23, 1991, in a black steamer trunk in the East River near Randalls Island. Her ex-husband identified her corpse.

Eight days later, the body of Mary Ellen DeLuca, twenty-two, of Valley Stream, Long Island, was discovered. It had been discarded on grass clippings in a field used as an illegal dump in upstate Cornwall, New York, not far from West Point. She wore only a bra.

At the time, state police had no idea who the young woman was. They checked records but DeLuca had never been arrested, and so no fingerprints were on file. After a donation came from a Cornwall resident, Mary Ellen DeLuca was buried in a private cemetery under a marker that read "Jane Doe." Meanwhile, her parents, Lois and Thomas DeLuca in Valley Stream, were praying every night that their daughter would walk through the door.

Mary Ellen, they knew, had been struggling with a drug problem. A few years earlier she'd dropped out of Central High School in Valley Stream. Despite her best efforts to stay away from drugs, Mary Ellen kept relapsing, winding up in Queens crack houses.

Her family tried desperately to help. Mary Ellen's three sisters, Loriann, Justine, and Susan, watched her every move. Lois and Tom DeLuca forced their daughter into various drug programs—once they even grabbed her off the street, dragging her into their car and driving directly to a hospital in Staten Island. Mary Ellen was admitted, and remained in a rehabilitation program for nine days. When she was released, she swore that this time she really would stay clean. And for six months, she did.

On the evening of September 1, 1991, Mary Ellen went out with a group of girlfriends. It was Labor Day weekend. The DeLucas were cleaning up, following an evening barbecue. Mary Ellen was planning to cap the night with dancing at J. Sprat's Dining Saloon in Island Park. It was a favorite night spot of hers.

But that night there wasn't any dancing— just football games on the large-screen TVs. Mary Ellen and her friends headed to Huey's, a nearby bar. A few of her girlfriends dropped Mary Ellen at home around 11:00 P.M. She waved goodbye.

But she never made it into the house. After her friend's car disappeared from sight, Mary Ellen went in search of drugs. That night, the hunger was too much to fight.

Somewhere along the way, Mary Ellen DeLuca encountered Joel Rifkin. Her family still can't believe she would sell her body, not to him, not to anyone. But perhaps the lure of drugs can be more powerful than any family-learned values. In any case, it doesn't change the terrible truth: Lois and Tom DeLuca's second youngest child died at the hands of Joel Rifkin.

When she didn't show up that night, Mary Ellen's parents reported her missing. They figured she had relapsed. It wasn't the first time she'd disappeared.

But as days turned into weeks, the De-Lucas knew this time was different. Yet they never gave up hope. They installed caller ID on their telephone. They took Mary Ellen's photograph to the drug dens she used to frequent in Queens. Sometimes, people would say they'd seen Mary Ellen, and the DeLucas' hopes would soar.

Shortly after Joel Rifkin was arrested, police released a report on all of his suspected victims. The victim from Cornwall, New York, they said, was a Valley Stream woman.

Friends and family of the DeLucas began to call, trying to prepare Lois and Tom for heartbreaking news. But Mary Ellen's parents refused to believe it.

"It can't be my daughter," Lois DeLuca kept repeating. "She couldn't have been lying up there for two years."

Not even when reporters showed up at the house did Lois DeLuca give up. Not even when she learned that the state police had released her daughter's name.

"It isn't my daughter," she told the press. "It isn't."

Her husband telephoned the state police in upstate New York, near where the Cornwall body had been found. He was angry.

"Are you releasing my daughter's name for any reason?" he asked.

And that's when Tom DeLuca learned that Mary Ellen's driver's license had been found in Joel Rifkin's bedroom. Investigators, the cop told him, were on their way to talk to the family.

"We'll wait," Tom DeLuca said quietly. He hung up the phone.

Turning to his wife and daughters, he told them about the license. His youngest child, Susan, broke down in his arms. "No, God, no, God, no," she sobbed.

But Tom and Lois DeLuca did not cry. To cry meant they had given up. Mary Ellen's parents were not ready to do that yet.

When troopers arrived about a half hour later, Lois and Tom wouldn't listen to them at first. They told the police that someone was almost positive he had seen their daughter just a few months ago in Queens. Another man was pretty sure he'd borrowed a dollar from her. The driver's license was no proof anyway. Mary Ellen had sold her license for drug money in the past.

And the time. It had been two years. How could her body lie unidentified for so long? How could this be possible?

The troopers gently assured the DeLucas that they wouldn't be there if they weren't sure. The Cornwall body was indeed Mary Ellen.

When the troopers and reporters finally left, Lois and Tom held each other for a long time.

At last they knew the truth. There was work to do—to make funeral preparations for their child. But right now, the couple could only cry. "I want my baby," Lois kept whispering. "I want her home."

The funeral for Mary Ellen DeLuca took place a week later. It was a hot Saturday. Members of the Sons of Italy Lodge in Queens, where Tom DeLuca is a member, carried the casket. At the Blessed Sacrament Catholic Church, Father John Dillon asked the more than four hundred mourners to pray also for Joel Rifkin's other victims.

"I don't think there are many words to fully capture the array of thoughts and feelings and emotions all clashing within our souls at the same time," the pastor said.

The service ended at the Cemetery of Holy Rood in Westbury.

At almost exactly the same time, another young woman was laid to rest about thirty miles away. Lorraine Orvieto's driver's license also had been found in Joel Rifkin's bedroom.

He'd strangled her a few months after Mary Ellen. In December 1991, about two years after he began to kill, Rifkin bought four fifty-five-gallon drums. He needed a new way to dispose of bodies. He was up to five by now—the two he'd mutilated plus Jacobs, Lee, and DeLuca.

A few days before Christmas, he went looking for his next victim.

She was Lorraine Orvieto, age twenty-eight.

Lorriane grew up in Stony Brook, the only daughter of Florence and Richard Orvieto. She was a good student, excelling in math and track. On weekends, she and her friends went dancing at the local teen center. She was tiny—just four feet eleven—but she loved to play basketball.

As a teenager, Lorraine began to suffer from depression. She went on medication, and for a while she improved. She was a cheerleader in high school and had such good grades she managed to graduate a year early, in 1980. She attended Suffolk Community College for a year, and then transfered to the C. W. Post campus of Long Island University, taking accounting classes at night. To pay for school, Lorraine ran a successful housekeeping service. With her earnings, she even bought a car. On weekends she went out with friends. They'd go dancing at Club 500 in Patchogue or Whispers in Smithtown.

But after she graduated from college, Lorraine's depression grew worse. She was working for a Manhattan accounting firm and the pressure was intense. The hours around tax season were brutal. Lorraine could no longer cope.

She quit. She tried to restart her housekeeping business but business was slow. Then, she heard through the grapevine that her ex-boyfriend was getting married. In fact, all of her friends seemed to be getting married.

Lorraine Orvieto sank into a serious depression. Doctors diagnosed her as a manic-depressive. They prescribed antidepressant drugs.

It wasn't enough. By then, Lorraine Orvieto had found an instant but deadly respite from her depression: she started taking crack. Eventually, she worked the streets of Brentwood and Bellport, Long Island, to support her habit. She lived off and on in a rooming house riddled with crack dealers.

In November of 1991 she was admitted to Kings Park Psychiatric Center, and a month later she was moved to an outpatient group home in Bay Shore, Long Island. But on December 20, 1991, Lorraine called her family and said she was going through a difficult time and wouldn't be seeing them for a while. They never heard from her again.

After Lorraine disappeared, her mother, Florence, called police and even visited psychics, restless for any news on her daughter. She filed a missing person's report and went to One Police Plaza in Manhattan to search through pictures of unidentified bodies. She wrote more than 150 letters to hospitals. She even tried to get the TV show *Unsolved Mysteries* to do a story on Lorraine's disappearance. In a spiral notebook, she kept a log of all of her attempts to find her daughter.

Florence Orvieto saved her daughter's Christmas presents—a sweater and an umbrella. They remained untouched, still wrapped in brightly colored paper. Deep down, she and her husband suspected their child was dead. Lorraine would have called. She always did.

In December 1992, almost a year to the day after Lorraine vanished, her family gathered at St. James Catholic Church to pray that they would learn of her whereabouts. When they gathered there again seven months later, it was for Lorraine's funeral.

Lorraine's name had been released about five days after Joel Rifkin's capture. Her best friend, Susanne Averso, heard it announced on the eleven o'clock news. The two young women had met in accounting class in college. Lorraine had been a bridesmaid in Susanne's wedding.

That night, Susanne cried for hours. She couldn't stop thinking of what she'd heard: that Lorraine had been one of three victims found stuffed in steel drums, floating in New York waters the previous summer. The drum that held Lorraine's body was discovered stuck in a pier in Coney Island Creek. For about a month, a fisherman had been using it to stand on. Then, on July 11, 1992, seven months after she was killed, the fisherman looked inside. The body had decomposed to the point that only a partial skeleton remained.

At Lorraine's funeral in Setauket, Long Island, her twenty-four-year-old brother, Danny, carried a single pink flower. The Reverend Joseph Mundy talked about the church service the previous December, and the prayers.

"Those prayers have been answered—not the way we wanted them to be answered, but they've been answered," Mundy said. "The struggle for Lorraine is over now."

Chapter 8

IN April 1991, about two years after he killed his first victim, Joel Rifkin leased a small plot of land from Kev's Landscaping Design and Tree Service of Hicksville. He told the owner, Kevin Seck, that he needed a place to store his trailer and gardening equipment. He didn't tell him he needed somewhere to stash bodies, too.

Seck offered Rifkin a fenced-in pen, twenty feet by fifty feet, for four hundred dollars a month. Rifkin signed a contract. He gave Seck a fifty-dollar deposit.

A few days later, Seck was taken aback when he saw Rifkin's equipment. His trailer was old and broken. He had outdated spreaders and a junky lawn mower.

Some landscaper, Seck thought.

Over the summer, Rifkin dropped by the pen several times a week. Now and then he stopped to talk with Seck. He always asked for pointers on operating a landscaping business.

"How do you do it?" Rifkin would ask. "I keep losing all my customers."

Seck tried to be encouraging. "You got to work with it," he'd say. "It takes time. And lots of work."

Seck didn't say what he was thinking—that Rifkin seemed lazy and unreliable, and that his equipment was a mess. To his brother, Tim, who also worked in the landscaping business, Kevin Seck scoffed at the idea of Joel Rifkin, a landscaper. "The guy's a lawn mower," he said. "He can't even keep his clients just cutting their grass. He doesn't have the necessary tools, his truck's a wreck, he's not licensed with a landscaping association. No certification. No insurance. He doesn't even have a name on his truck. He doesn't even have business cards."

* * *

By midsummer Rifkin had dropped behind in his rent. Clearly, his mind was elsewhere. By then he'd killed his third victim—Barbara Jacobs.

Rifkin began paying in smaller installments. Some months he skipped completely. By fall, Seck had had enough.

"You got to pay your rent," he told Rifkin sternly, "or I'm going to lock up your gate. You've got to pay."

"I will," Rifkin told him. "I should be getting another job this week."

Seck had heard it before. "If you don't pay by the end of the week, I'm really going to lock your gate," he said.

Seck and his brother, Tim, tried to work out a deal: they offered to buy Rifkin's red Ford dump truck. As it was, Rifkin had told them that he was having trouble meeting the payments.

"How much are you looking for?" asked Tim.

Rifkin never gave a direct answer. "I'll let you know," he said vaguely.

Kevin Seck began to call the Rifkin house several times a week. He tried Joel's private line, but Rifkin never answered the phone. Seck left countless messages. When he called the main number, Seck usually reached Jeanne Rifkin.

"Your son hasn't paid for a couple of months," he'd say.

Jeanne Rifkin sounded sympathetic. "That's not like him," she'd say. "I'll talk to him. I'm sure he'll take care of it."

By December 1991 Rifkin told Seck that he was closing his landscaping business. He promised to pay the seven hundred dollars he still owed.

"I don't have any work," Rifkin said. "I've got one possibility I'm working on. If this job comes through, I'll take care of the rest." Rifkin made one more payment of a hundred dollars and then disappeared. The next time Seck heard about him Joel Rifkin was on the front page of all four New York City newspapers.

Within days, Seck learned the grim details: that all along Rifkin had been storing bodies on Seck's land. By the time Rifkin left Kev's in December 1991, his gruesome tally had been at least six.

About the same time, Rifkin bought the fifty-five-gallon drums. Over the next few months he strangled four more young women. He loaded their remains into the drums and threw them into New York City rivers. In addition to Lorraine Orvieto, there was Maryann Hollomon. Her corpse was found stuffed in a drum floating in Coney Island Creek on July 9, just two days before Lorraine Orvieto's. Holloman was thirty-nine, five foot four, and had lived in a single-room occupancy hotel in the East Village, home to drug addicts and prostitutes. Her credit cards were found in Rifkin's home; she was positively identified by dental records.

The third and fourth victims are still not identified. One has not even been found. She was stuffed in a drum and thrown into the Harlem River. The second body was found in a drum in Newtown Creek in Greenpoint, Brooklyn on May 13, 1992, about two months before Orvieto's and Hollomon's. At 11:30 A.M. that day, a sanitation worker spotted the drum floating in the creek, behind North Henry Street and Greenpoint Avenue. He saw a leg sticking out of it.

Half the body was decomposed, and toxicological tests indicated that traces of cocaine were in her system. Detectives in the Ninety-fourth Precinct thought the woman might have been a drug mule who had died of an overdose when condoms holding cocaine burst in her stomach. Later, they learned that Joel Rifkin had killed her sometime that winter.

In the spring of 1992, while the bodies of his four latest victims floated in the oil drums, the first two dismembered were still undiscovered, and the deaths of his first two victims, Barbara Jacobs and Yun Lee, remained a mystery, Joel Rifkin went back to agricultural school at SUNY Farmingdale. This time he was not permitted to apply for the matriculated program; he took uncredited classes instead.

He drifted in and out of classes, and spent hours working on his truck. By then, his driver's license had been suspended— again—after he failed to answer a summons.

In the evenings, Rifkin often drove to a video store in Uniondale and rented porno movies about prostitutes. The owner didn't think much about Joel Rifkin. One thing he did notice—Joel Rifkin never looked him in the eye.

In general, Rifkin's routine didn't vary much. Classes, working on the truck, stopping at the Apollo diner for lunch. He'd been a regular at the Apollo for several years. He always ordered the same meal—scrambled eggs, white toast, coffee. It came to $3.30. He left a fifteen-cent tip.

His waitress was almost always Judy Maltese. The short, energetic woman in a black-and-white uniform and white sneakers had been waiting tables for seventeen years. Her coworkers often joked that Judy Maltese had been waiting tables at the Apollo since before it even opened.

Maltese always sighed when she spotted Joel Rifkin. His fifteen-cent tips really bugged her. Each time, she was tempted to speak up.

One day, I'm going to just say, "Take your fifteen cents and keep it," she'd think.

Sometimes, she practiced what she'd say: I'll say, "Hey, take your fifteen cents, you need it more than me," she thought. Or else, "Don't leave anything if you're going to leave 15 cents. It's insulting."

But she never did. She knew the Apollo's owners, Bob and Louie, wouldn't like it.

And so she continued to serve Joel Rifkin. He never lingered; just stared into his plate, ate quickly, and left. Judy Maltese wondered about him.

* * *

In April 1992 Rifkin killed again. This time his victim was Iris Sanchez. She was twenty-five years old, the youngest of five siblings. Iris Sanchez had a little girl, an eight-year-old named Jolene, who lived with Sanchez's parents.

As a child, Sanchez had looked up to her big brothers and sisters, trying to emulate them. One of her sisters was a New York City housing cop. But later, as a teen, Iris Sanchez began to follow her friends. She got into drugs, and then prostitution. Despite several arrests and countless drug binges, Sanchez refused to move back with her family. They tried to get her into rehabilitation programs, but nothing stuck.

Iris always called home on holidays and on her daughter's birthday. But she felt her child was better off without a drug-addicted mother. So she stayed away.

After he killed Iris Sanchez, Joel Rifkin dropped her fully clothed body in a deserted field next to John F. Kennedy International Airport. It was pretty easy, actually. He lifted an old mattress lying nearby and threw it on top of the corpse.

For more than a year, the body decom-

posed under the mattress. During his interrogation, Joel Rifkin described where he had
left it. "I put it in the sand," he told Capers
and Louder. "Near Thurston Basin."

That's exactly were it was, about two hundred feet off Rockaway Boulevard, near the
water. The morning after Rifkin's arrest,
state police notified the Queens district attorney, who in turn called the Port Authority
police. That afternoon, cops searched the
field by helicopter. When they spotted a mattress, they slowly brought the helicopter
down. The spinning rotors blew away the
mattress. Port Authority cops looked down
and saw a skeleton.

There was still some hair on the head, and
the body was still wearing a dark dress with
large white polka dots. And one sock. Rifkin
had told investigators the woman was wearing just one shoe.

When he left Iris Sanchez's body under the
mattress that spring night, Joel Rifkin's
cold-blooded count was at least six dead.

Then, on May 25, 1992, he met Anna
Lopez.

Chapter 9

NINE days later, on June 3, 1992, Anna Lopez didn't pick up her monthly social security check. Her mother knew at once that she was dead.

Ever since her daughter became addicted to crack six years earlier, María Alonso knew she couldn't count on Annie for much. But she also knew that Annie would never disappear and not call. And she knew the social security check Annie received on the third of every month meant a guaranteed visit. On that day, Annie would arrive early in the morning and settle down at the kitchen table, waiting impatiently for the mail. How angry she got if the mailman was late!

It was then that María Alonso tried to reach her daughter. "Annie," she'd say, "you need to get your life together. You need to join the program. The drugs, Annie. You need to get clean."

"I will, Mommy," Annie always said. "I will."

Sometimes, late at night, María thought back to a time when drugs hadn't claimed her daughter. Annie had been a happy child. María could still picture her skipping to school, clasping her big sister Claudia's hand. María had been protective of her girls. She remembered the first time she let Annie and Claudia walk the three blocks to school by themselves. As the girls hurried down the block, excited by their newfound freedom, María ran to the roof of her apartment building. From her vantage point, she watched carefully to see if her children waited at the corner and looked both ways.

María Alonso didn't know what went wrong. What weakness in Annie had caused her to turn to drugs? she wondered. María knew she'd done her best to keep her three daughters off the streets. No mother had tried harder.

But early on there had been troubling

signs. It seemed as if Annie had no self-confidence at all. Then, when she was thirteen, Annie tried to commit suicide.

María could never forget that night. She had gone to play bridge, leaving her three daughters at home: Claudia, Annie, and Monica, the baby.

It was Annie's turn to do dishes. All the Alonso girls knew their mother didn't take kindly to excuses; she expected her daughters to pitch in around the apartment. The Alonso home was always immaculate.

But that night, Annie procrastinated for hours. She had a friend visiting. The dishes could wait.

Big sister Claudia was not so understanding. As the oldest, she felt a responsibility to see that chores got done. She kept the pressure on Annie.

"It's your turn," Claudia kept saying. "Mommy's going to be mad."

"I'll do it," Annie insisted. "In a minute."

Finally, Claudia lost her patience. Annie had been chatting with her girlfriend all evening. María would be home within the hour. Claudia yelled at her little sister. Then, she slapped her across the face.

"Mommy's going to be so mad at you," Claudia announced.

Humiliated, Annie ran to the bathroom and slammed the door. She stayed locked inside for a long time. Inexplicably, she swallowed a fistful of pills, medication she had been taking since she had been in contact with someone who had tuberculosis.

María Alonso believes it was the embarrassment of being scolded in front of a friend that pushed Annie over the edge. She thinks her daughter had a weakness, an extreme sensitivity that made her easily fall apart. If there was something more going on with Annie at that time, María never understood it. All she knew was that she did her best to be a good parent.

María Alonso remembers arriving home that night, shortly before midnight. The dishes were done. The children were sleeping. She went to bed.

Forty-five minutes later Annie stood at the foot of her bed. "Mommy, Mommy," she moaned.

María snapped on the light. Annie's face was blue. She collapsed on the carpet and went into convulsions.

María called an ambulance. Annie was

rushed to Kings County Hospital. María watched in horror as doctors placed electrical paddles on Annie's chest and delivered shocks to stimulate the heart. She saw her daughter's body jerk violently.

These days, María Alonso thinks about how her daughter died twice.

The first time, though, a miracle happened and Annie came back. In the hospital, the morning after she swallowed the pills, Annie opened her eyes.

"Mommy, where am I?" she asked. "What happened?"

María could hardly see through her tears. "Where do you live?" she asked softly.

"Brooklyn."

"What are your sisters' names?"

"Claudia and Monica."

María Alonso thanked God. He had answered her prayers.

When Annie was released from Kings County, doctors reminded María to bring her daughter in regularly for follow-up visits. Convulsions were serious, they explained. There was always a possibility of brain damage.

But once she got home, Annie refused to

return to the hospital. She said she wanted to forget what had happened.

"I don't need it," she said. "I'm fine."

Looking back, María Alonso wonders if Annie did have brain damage. Maybe that's why she didn't think straight, María often thought as she lay in bed, trying to make sense of her daughter's life and death. Maybe that's why she turned to drugs.

Over the years, María Alonso shared her theory with her sister Blanca, who lived around the corner. They'd sit in the kitchen for hours, smoking cigarettes and talking about Annie.

"I feel guilty," María often began. "If I'd insisted that Annie go to the doctor for those follow-up visits . . ."

Blanca always cut her off. She reminded her sister that she had been a good mother. Annie's drug problem was not her fault. "It's not you," Blanca would say earnestly. "It's the environment. You can't fight the environment."

María Alonso would always agree, nodding wearily. "You see things coming," she'd say softly. "You see it coming and you try to warn them, try to make them see the light. I tried. I tried so hard to keep my girls off drugs."

María Alonso did see it coming. When Annie dropped out of school in the eleventh grade, María pleaded on her knees.

"The only way you'll get ahead in life is to finish school," she said, weeping. "Please, Annie. Don't throw away your life. Go to school. What else will you do with your life?"

"I'll go back, Mommy," Annie said. "Just not now. But I will. I promise."

When Annie was twenty she married José Lopez. They had a daughter, Venus. María Alonso had mixed feelings about her son-in-law. He was kind, smart, and a good husband. She knew José Lopez loved her daughter. And Annie adored him.

But José Lopez had a drug problem, and before long, Annie was doing drugs too. A few years after they married, José was arrested for selling guns. He spent six months in prison; Annie wrote to him every day. She sent pictures of herself working at a sweater factory. On the back she wrote, "This is me at my job. I am working hard for both of us. I don't look too cute here but at least you could see what I am doing while you're away.

I love you much, darling. Te Amo, Papi."
Beneath the words she placed a lipstick kiss.

For a while after José Lopez was paroled
things seemed to be going well. María
Alonso was hopeful that the bad times were
over. Then, shortly before Christmas of
1985, José Lopez died of a cocaine overdose.
Little Venus was just four years old.

At the funeral, María held her daughter,
rocking slowly. "You will get better with
time, Annie," she whispered. "You will get
on with your life. It will be alright."

It never was. Annie's grief was overwhelming, and she quickly turned to crack. Almost
overnight, she was an addict.

María didn't know about the drugs. But
she knew her daughter was suffering. For
months she tried to convince Annie to move
back home.

"Live with me," María pleaded. "I have the
room."

"No, Mommy," Annie always said. "I want
to make it on my own."

But drugs were siphoning all her money.
Even though she worked at the sweater factory, and tried to earn extra cleaning offices,
Annie was always broke. A year after her
husband died, she hit bottom. She'd blown

all her money on crack and couldn't pay the rent. She and Venus were evicted from their apartment. At last, Annie confided in her sister. She told Claudia about the drugs.

Claudia was adamant. "Annie, you've got to talk to Mommy," she said. "She has to know."

"I can't," Annie said, sighing. "I just can't tell her this."

"You have to," Claudia insisted. "Mommy is the only one who can help you."

Annie had little choice. She told her mother about the crack.

At first María Alonso was angry. She raised her voice in frustration.

"This was my battle all my life," she said sharply. "To keep my daughters off drugs."

But María recognized the pain in her daughter's eyes. She knew how difficult this was for Annie. She softened. She leaned across the kitchen table and took her child's hand.

"It's not too late," she said earnestly. "There's help. Let's go get help, Annie."

Annie entered Monticello Hospital and spent a week in detox. Then she called her mother.

"Mommy, I'm ready to go home now," she said.

María felt a sense of dread. For the past week she had been talking to friends about Annie's addiction. Everyone had warned her that Annie had a long way to go before she was ready to return home.

"No, Annie," María said slowly. "You have to go to a rehabilitation center. You have to stay away from here so you'll be strong when you come home. You're not ready. Stay there. I'll take care of Venus. I'll visit you every week. I'll bring you anything you want. Please, Annie. Please."

"No, Mommy," Annie said solemnly. "I learned my lesson. I'll never use again. I promise."

Two days after Annie returned home, she relapsed.

It was just before Christmas of 1986, a little over a year after José Lopez's death. Annie was going to a party with her sisters and cousins. She looked so pretty. María beamed when she saw her.

"You look beautiful, Annie," María said. "Are you going to eat here?"

"No, Mommy, I'll eat with my friends."

María Alonso turned to the stove for a

Joel Rifkin, the Long Island man who allegedly killed 18 prostitutes, shown in his 1977 senior yearbook picture from East Meadow High School. *(AP/Wide World)*

New York State Police Captain Walter Heesch addresses reporters outside Troop L headquarters in East Farmingdale, Wednesday, June 30, 1993 — just two days after Rifkin was apprehended. *(AP/Wide World/Mike Alexander)*

Joel Rifkin arrives at court in Mineola, NY, July 15, 1993, where he was charged with the death of a woman found strangled in the back of his pickup truck. *(AP/Wide World)*

Police investigators examine the remains of Iris Sanchez, whose body was found near Kennedy Airport.
(AP/Wide World/Mike Alexander)

An unidentified photographer approaches the spot where a body was found in Southampton, N.Y., after suspected serial killer Joel Rifkin led police to the spot on June 29th.
(AP/Wide World/ Joe Tabacca)

The Rifkin family home on Garden Street in East Meadow, New York. *(Maria Eftimiades)*

Joel Rifkin's sister, Jan, and mother, Jeanne, leave their East Meadow home en route to his arraignment on June 29th. (Newsday/*Dick Kraus)*

Margarita Gonzalez, right, looks at a picture of her daughter Jenny Soto, whose body was found seven months ago beside the Harlem River. Soto is believed to be one of Joel Rifkin's victims. *(AP/Wide World/Malcolm Clarke)*

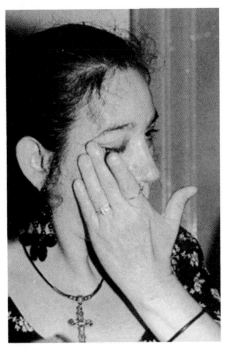

Margarita Gonzalez wipes away a tear as she talks with reporters at the Mineola, NY courthouse on July 15th where Joel Rifkin pleaded not guilty to murder charges.
(AP/Wide World/ Mike Alexander)

Maria Alonso, right, and Margarita Gonzalez hold hands and wipe tears from their eyes during a taping of the "Sally Jessy Raphael" television show. "I want to see the face of the monster who took my daughter's life," Alonso said. "I want to spit on it." *(AP/Wide World)*

A coalition of women's groups stands outside the Jack the Ripper Pub in New York's Greenwich Village, charging that because the victims of alleged serial killer Joel Rifkin were prostitutes, their disappearances went unnoticed until he was arrested. *(AP/Wide World/Jim Cooper)*

Joel Rifkin paid prostitute Charlotte Webb twice for sex but never displayed any hostility: "He said he liked me," Charlotte mused. "I guess that's why I'm still alive." *(Maria Eftimiades)*

minute. When she looked back, Annie was gone.

She must have gone to Blanca's apartment, María thought.

But Annie wasn't there. She was walking down Atlantic Avenue headed for a crack house about ten blocks away. She didn't return home for days. Her Christmas presents went unopened that year.

Until the day she died, Annie's life never improved. She'd spend a few days at home and then disappear. Crack controlled her completely.

In the beginning, she took Venus with her to buy drugs. The little girl was just five.

"Don't expose her," María pleaded. "Why take your child, Annie? Don't. Don't take her."

Annie paid no attention. María was scared. She'd read in the newspapers about mothers selling their children to men for drugs. She couldn't believe Annie would do that. But she didn't trust her. And Venus needed protection.

María made up her mind. One night she pulled Annie aside. Her voice was firm. "If you take Venus again," she said, "I'll call the Bureau of Child Welfare. And I mean it."

She did. The next day, when Annie took Venus with her to buy drugs, María called city officials. Early the next morning a social worker appeared at the door.

Annie told the social worker the truth. She admitted that she had a drug problem. She said she was trying to fight it.

The social worker listened patiently. Then she laid down rules.

"You cannot take Venus with you anymore," she said firmly. "Venus stays under your mother's care. And you can no longer live here. If you want to see your child, you must be in a program."

But Annie didn't go into a program. For the next few years she lived off and on with friends or in a crack house. To earn money for drugs, she became a prostitute.

Sometimes María and Venus saw Annie when they walked down Atlantic Avenue to the laundromat, or to go for lunch at a Greek restaurant that Venus liked.

Annie always hugged them and smiled. She's such an actress, María would think. Always pretending that nothing is wrong.

But a mother knows. A mother knows her child's pain.

Annie was so thin. At five foot two, she was under one hundred pounds. It hurt María to see her daughter that way. When Annie arrived on the third of every month to pick up her social security check, María implored her to eat.

"You don't eat, Annie," she'd tell her. "Just look at you."

"I will, Mommy," Annie would say. "I will."

Annie would artfully change the subject. She asked about the family—her sisters, aunts, and cousins. She always wanted to know about Venus.

When the mail arrived Annie would slip the check into her pocket and quickly kiss her mother goodbye. The money meant vials of crack. María Alonso knew it.

"Take care of Venus," Annie would always say as she left. "And take care of my plant."

In 1989, Annie had another child, a daughter she named Salana. The little girl lived with her father. Then, three years later, Annie got pregnant again.

This time she didn't know who the father was. As her pregnancy progressed, Annie began to talk more seriously about getting into a drug rehabilitation program. She said she was tired. She was getting older. It was time to turn her life around.

María Alonso nodded enthusiastically. Always, she'd stayed hopeful. For the first time, her daughter seemed genuinely ready. Perhaps this would be it. Perhaps Annie would at last break the addiction.

While she was pregnant, Annie knitted an outfit for the baby. She spoke with her aunt Virginia, her mother's younger sister, about taking care of the child.

"When you get clean, you can have the baby back," her aunt promised. "Get clean, Annie. Do it for your baby."

The baby was born addicted to crack. But she was a good size—seven pounds, seven ounces. Venus picked the baby's name—Megan.

In the hospital, Annie fed the baby and rocked her. After a week she was ready to be released, but Megan wasn't. Doctors told Annie that her new daughter had to stay in the hospital for detox.

Annie felt terrible leaving Megan behind. She felt bad that her baby was suffering. She thought of her aunt's promise. Get clean.

Raise your child. It was time, Annie decided. This time, she really began to believe she could turn things around.

María Alonso met Annie at the hospital the day she was released. It was Valentine's Day, 1992. Mother and daughter walked hand in hand to the corner. Annie had an appointment with a social worker. She was going to take the bus.

"I'm going to go into a program, Mommy," she said. "I am."

"That's good, Annie," María said. "This is the best time for you. You were in the hospital, so you're off drugs for seven days. Your system is clean. It's your mind you have to fight."

Annie nodded. The bus pulled to the curb. She leaned over to give her mother a hug.

"Annie, what do you want to eat tonight?" María asked. "Shall I get an Oven Stuffer and cranberry sauce? Your favorite? What should I make, Annie?"

Annie smiled, only the smile seemed sad. All the love, all the promises, all the plans. Crack was stronger than everything.

"I like everything you make, Mommy," she said softly. "Anything you want."

María Alonso suddenly felt cold. Annie

wasn't coming home tonight. She knew her daughter. She knew the pattern.

"Annie, you're coming back?" María said. "Are you sure, Annie?"

"I will, Mommy. I promise."

That night, María Alonso glazed the chicken with cranberry sauce. A few hours later she lay her head on the kitchen table and cried. Annie hadn't come home. A short time later, she didn't show up to pick up her social security check.

Chapter 10

JOEL Rifkin told police that he picked up Anna Lopez on May 25, 1992. He paid her for sex, and then he strangled her.

By now, he'd used up all his oil drums. He needed a new way to dispose of his latest victim. So he loaded Annie's body in the back of his pickup and drove upstate to Putnam County. He found a spot—along the Park-n-Ride off Interstate 84 in Brewster. He didn't bother to bury María Alonso's child. He dumped her body in the woods.

Before he left, Rifkin unfastened one of Annie Lopez's gold earrings. He put it in his pocket and drove home. Less than twenty-four hours later, on Memorial Day, a driver who stopped to urinate found the body.

Local cops took a photograph of the corpse and made hundreds of flyers, posting them in rest stops along the highway. They removed the single gold earring and placed it in an evidence bag.

When Annie didn't appear on June 3, María Alonso turned to her sister, Blanca. "I told you before," she said slowly. "If Annie doesn't pick up this check, she's dead."

Blanca tried to be optimistic. "She's probably sleeping," she said. "You know she can sleep for a long time. Days even. We'll see what happens tomorrow. Don't worry."

The next day there was still no sign of Annie. María and Blanca went to the Seventy-fifth Precinct.

María explained the situation. She told the police officer at the front desk that her daughter was a crack addict, but that she always came home for her social security check. This month, she hadn't shown up. Something had to be wrong.

The officer on duty shrugged.

"She probably met someone and went to the Bahamas," he said.

* * *

For the next month María Alonso canvassed the neighborhood. She went to the crack house, seeking out Annie's friends. A young woman there told her that she, too, was worried.

"I'm scared," the young woman said. "I haven't seen Annie in weeks. It isn't like her to disappear like this."

On the street, María showed her daughter's photographs—the ones before crack, when Annie's eyes were bright, her smile real. A few people said they'd seen Annie Lopez. On the street. In the crack house. Talking to friends.

It gave María hope. But deep down, she knew it couldn't be true.

She checked the city morgue, the jails and hospitals. July 3 came and went. A second social security check went unclaimed. That's when María knew for sure.

She returned to the Seventy-fifth Precinct. This time she met with a detective. He was more sympathetic.

"Ma'am, it doesn't sound good," he told her kindly. "Go tomorrow to One Police Plaza. They're going to show you photos."

María turned to her sister. "Blanca, would you go with me?" she asked.

The two women took the subway to lower Manhattan the next day. "I know Annie's dead," María said wearily. "All I want is to find her body so she can have a decent burial."

In a large, windowless room on the eleventh floor, police jotted down Annie's height, weight, and hair color. They pulled out several heavy books of photos. The bodies in the pictures fit Annie's general description.

María looked at two pictures and closed the book. She began to cry. "Blanca, can you look for me?" she asked.

Her sister gave her a hug. "Of course," she said.

For the next hour Blanca searched through the pages of the book. María sat motionless a few feet away. Her eyes never left her sister's face. She knew she would see it in Blanca's eyes if Annie Lopez's photograph was in that book.

Finally, Blanca closed the last book. The policewoman on duty looked up and smiled gently at María Alonso.

"Well, ma'am, you have to feel better," she said. "She's not dead because she's not in the pictures."

María tried to return the smile. She was so tired. She couldn't think straight anymore.

The police officer wanted to help—she knew that. But the truth was María didn't feel better, she felt worse. Somebody probably threw her body somewhere and she's rotting away, she thought to herself. Now I'll never find her. If she's not here, where is she?

Blanca reached for her sister's hand. The two women thanked the officers and began to leave. At that moment—María Alonso still doesn't know why—she turned and looked at the wall behind her. Posted on a board were dozens of Missing Persons flyers. María's eyes went directly to the state police flyer from Putnam County—with the photo of Anna Lopez.

She walked slowly to the wall. She stared intently.

Finally, she broke the silence.

"Blanca," she cried. "That's her!"

The police officer shook her head. "No," she said. "That's some woman they found a long time ago in Brewster, New York."

María Alonso read the description. It was wrong. It listed the woman as five foot four; Annie was five foot two. It said she had dark hair. Annie's was light brown. It didn't matter.

"I'm telling you, that's my daughter," María said. "It's Annie."

The officer called her supervisor. "This lady thinks the lady from Brewster is her daughter," she said.

The supervisor pulled down the flyer. "Do you have a picture of your daughter?" he asked.

María pulled out several photos. The cop chose one and made an enlarged copy. He turned the copy and the flyer upside down and began examining the images carefully.

"It's not your daughter," he said finally. "The noses don't match. They're not the same."

But María refused to give up. Later she decided that Annie must have wanted her to know the truth. She didn't want me to leave without claiming her body, María thought. She wanted me to fight for her.

And so Annie's mother did. "I'm telling you," she said. "I don't know how she died. But people when they die, their features do change. I gave birth to her. I know."

The cop was equally stubborn.

"It's not your daughter," he kept repeating. "It's not."

Finally, María Alonso slammed her hand down on the table. "It *is* my daughter," she said, "Don't you want to do your job?"

The cop gave up. He reached for the phone. He spoke for a few minutes and then turned to María and her sister. He told them that a state trooper would pick them up the next day and take them to Brewster to identify the body.

During the ride upstate the next morning, María Alonso prayed. If she's dead, she's dead, she thought. I just want this to be over.

They went first to the local police station and answered questions about Annie—about her drug addiction, and when they'd last seen her. Then, the two women were driven to a funeral home. It only took one look.

"A mother knows her child," María whispered as she touched the face of her Annie. "When they go to sleep you look at them. You know every little detail on their face. A mother knows her child."

For a long time, María Alonso had believed that crack would someday kill her daughter. But when police told her that Annie Lopez had been strangled, the petite, soft-spoken woman became obsessed with finding her child's killer.

María took to the streets. Carrying Annie's photograph, she went up and down Atlantic

Avenue, in and out of drug dens. Dealers and users became accustomed to seeing the dark-haired Puerto Rican woman. They understood her pain. They promised to help.

"Keep your eyes and ears open," she'd always say as she was leaving. "Because if the killer is someone from around here, sooner or later someone's going to talk."

María's oldest daughter, Claudia, pleaded with her to stay home. The idea of her mother in drug houses frightened her.

"Let the police do it," she said. "Please, Mommy. It's not safe."

María hardly heard her. "It's someone from around here," she said. "I know it is. I have to find Annie's killer."

Now and then she was given bits of information. Someone, she was told, had been on the streets, bragging about having killed Anna Lopez. It took a few weeks before María tracked down a name. For the next few months she appeared at the crack house at various times, trying to find the man. After a while, others told her no. It wasn't him after all.

Sometimes, María thought about the earring. Cops had told her that a single earring was found on her daughter's body.

"That earring," María told her sister.

"That other earring's someplace. It's going to link her killer, Blanca. I'm not psychic, but these are feelings that mothers get."

Some days, María didn't have the strength to search. She kept thinking back: just when Annie had seemed ready to join a program and turn her life around. Some nights, it was too much to bear.

"She was going to do it this time, Blanca," Maria would weep. "Just when she was ready. I believe in God. He always answers my prayers. If he could have given her one more chance. One more. This time, I know she was ready to do it."

María Alonso and her sister spent many long nights talking about Annie. Blanca understood her sister's determination to find the killer. She knew it was the only way María could finally put her daughter to rest.

María Alonso was in her living room on the evening of Monday, June 28. She put on the 11:00 P.M. news.

The lead story took her breath away. She listened intently. She looked at Joel Rifkin's face as he was led out of state trooper headquarters in handcuffs. And she knew.

María ran around the corner and up the stairs. She banged loudly on Blanca's door.

"That man killed my daughter," she screamed. "Blanca. That man from Long Island. He did it. He killed Annie."

She was right. The next morning, the name Anna Lopez was released by police. Blanca heard it on the radio. She immediately called her sister.

"You were right," Blanca said. "Your daughter's name was on the list of the victims."

María Alonso called the detectives upstate who had been handling Annie's case. She asked for Investigator Card. He had always been kind to her.

The investigator was surprised. He hadn't heard anything yet about a link between Joel Rifkin and Annie Lopez. But he promised to find out. He said he would call state troopers on Long Island and phone her back right away.

Within minutes, he did. It was confirmed. Rifkin had admitted killing Anna Lopez. Also, the missing earring had been located in Joel Rifkin's bedroom.

"We are one hundred percent sure that he killed your daughter," said Investigator

Card. "At least now, Mrs. Alonso, you can rest."

But she couldn't. The media blitz was just beginning.

Chapter 11

ON Tuesday, June 29, the day after his arrest, Joel Rifkin was arraigned in First District Court in Hempstead. About half an hour before the proceedings began, he met his attorney for the first time.

Rifkin was seated, handcuffed, in the detention area, wearing the white jumpsuit given to him by police the night before. Court officers led Robert Sale into the small room.

"How are you?" the attorney asked.

Rifkin got right to the point. "I need my glasses," he said, exasperated. "They've been taken. Can you help me get them back?"

The attorney said he would try. He told

Rifkin that he would broach the issue during arraignment.

Rifkin looked relieved. "I can't function without them," he added. "I'm getting a migraine headache."

Sale began to explain what Rifkin could expect in the near future. He told his client that, for now, he was being arraigned on second-degree murder charges in connection with the body found in the back of his pickup. An indictment in the next few weeks was likely.

Sale informed Rifkin that he did not plan to ask for bail. It was extremely unlikely that such a request would be granted. If it were, bail would be set so high it would be impossible for the Rifkin family to meet it.

Rifkin didn't respond. He knew his mother didn't have much money. He also knew his attorney was right; the chances of an affordable bail were nil.

Sale said he'd already talked to Jeanne Rifkin earlier that morning. She and Jan would be in the courtroom. It was important, Sale told his client, that the Rifkin family appear supportive.

After the arraignment, Rifkin would be taken to the Nassau County Correctional Facility in East Meadow. Sale would ask that he be placed in protective custody, away from other inmates. Sale told Rifkin that the judge and prosecutor would have no objection. Protective custody was standard in high-profile cases. And cases didn't get much more high-profile than this.

"Are you being treated alright?" Sale asked.

Rifkin said he was. He added, though, that he was upset about the media spotlight on his family. When he'd phoned his mother last night from police headquarters she said reporters had been camped on the sidewalk all evening. Her phone hadn't stopped ringing. Some of the tabloid television shows had even offered money for Jeanne and Jan Rifkin's exclusive story.

Sale had already heard the complaints from Jeanne Rifkin. He stressed that it was important to remain silent and not to talk to the media. A criminal case, he explained, must be tried in the courts. Not in the newspapers.

It was 9:30 A.M. The bailiff called the court to order. Judge John Kingston was presiding.

Jeanne and Jan Rifkin sat with Sale's partner Mark Groothuis in the third row. Jan wore a simple black top and skirt and red suede pumps; her mother had on purple pants and a white shirt embroidered with a butterfly. In her hands, Jeanne Rifkin clutched a red spiral notebook.

As Joel Rifkin entered the courtroom he looked around quickly. Without his glasses, everything was blurred. He thought he saw his mother and sister, but he couldn't be sure.

His wasn't the only arraignment that morning. Seven other prisoners were led in, two of whom were directed to sit next to him. Rifkin raised his legs and swiveled to the side as they scooted past. The man seated next to him gave him a sidelong look and moved an inch away. Joel Rifkin stared at the floor.

The clerk of the court spoke first.

THE CLERK: People versus Joel Rifkin.

MR. SALE: Good morning, Your Honor.

Your Honor, I would waive a reading of the information and, in view of the media attention to this matter, I am not going to ask the Court to set bail at this time. We would like to reserve our rights, at an appropriate time, to seek fair and reasonable bail.

I would ask this matter be postponed until July 6 for a conference in Part IX.

I have received a copy of the charge, singular charge, in this case together with the appropriate notices from the assistant district attorney.

I have a further application, Your Honor. I would ask my client be placed in protective custody at the Nassau County Correctional Facility and, also, that his glasses have been taken from him, as is required. However, he now has a migraine headache and needs his glasses to function. I would ask the authorities, if possible, after checking them out as required, if they could return them to him.

THE COURT: First of all, the request for protective custody is granted.

MR. SALE: Thank you, Judge.

THE COURT: The glasses are to be returned to the defendant and the application for a conference on July 6 in Part IX is granted.

I would like the record to note that defense counsel and the district attorney's office had a conference with the Court this morning prior to my taking the bench and defense counsel objected to the use of any television cameras, still photos, or audio in this arraignment.

Pursuant to the rules of this Court, unless there is unanimous consent, there cannot be any television, audio, or still photos. Therefore, none will be permitted in this court.

At that point Mark Groothuis motioned to Jeanne and Jan Rifkin. They stepped out into the aisle and walked to the front.

"Your Honor, I would also like to indicate that my client's mother and sister are present in court today as a sign of their support for Joel," Sale said.

And then it was over. Jeanne and Jan Rifkin waited until the press had filed out of the courtroom. They spoke quietly to Mark Groothuis. At one point, Jeanne Rifkin glanced at a courtroom artist's depiction of Joel.

Then she turned away.

A few minutes later, her son was led into a police van and taken to jail. As the van headed down Carman Avenue, it passed East Meadow High School. It had been sixteen years since Joel Rifkin graduated. The outcast had finally made his mark.

* * *

Back at the courthouse, reporters practically chased Rifkin's mother and sister as they hurried into a waiting white Jaguar. Robert Sale was left to face the media. He was quickly encircled. Reporters pressed so close the attorney could hardly move. Ignoring their questions, he held up his hand. "My office is two blocks away," he said. "If you want to come over, I'll be there by noon."

The crowd quickly dispersed. About two hours later some fifty reporters, photographers, and film crews assembled in the parking lot of Sale, Groothuis and Hirsch on Hilton Avenue. The journalists waited impatiently. They had questions. Lots of questions.

Inside his office, Sale was a bit uneasy. He'd had high-profile cases in the past, but nothing of this scope. When he stepped outside and began to speak, his voice quavered.

The reporters didn't care. They immediately hammered away.

"Mr. Sale, the assistant district attorney says your client is a serial killer," boomed Ralph Penza from New York's WNBC-TV.

Sale tried to be flip. "What do I know about serial killers?" he said. "It probably means he eats cornflakes for breakfast."

Reporters exchanged glances. The remark sounded inappropriate and disingenuous.

Sale tried again.

"Give the man his due," he said, his voice becoming more firm. "He's innocent until proven guilty. My client has been convicted in the newspapers already. It's almost impossible for him to get a fair trial because of the widespread publicity. He'd need a jury of twelve snails."

"Why didn't you ask for bail?" a reporter called out.

"It would be an exercise in futility," Sale replied. "The bail would be so high it would be tantamount to no bail. If John Wilkes Booth was on trial I don't think his lawyer would try to bail him out. We'd waste everyone's time at the bail hearing."

Sale then hinted at an insanity defense. He told the press that he had met with his client earlier that day. Joel, he said, had acted emotionally disturbed at times. "He gave some appropriate responses, and some inappropriate responses," he said.

When pressed further, Sale backed down. He had no intention of discussing a possible defense.

"We're not going to try this case in the

media," Sale said sharply. "The case will have
to proceed in court."

And the press conference was over.

The next morning, at 9:00 A.M., Sale drove to
Nassau County Correctional Facility and met
with his client. They talked for almost two
hours. When attorney-client visiting hours
were over, Sale offered Rifkin his home telephone number. "If you have any problems,
don't hesitate to call collect anytime," he
said. "You're no different from any other
client."

Later that day, Sale met individually with
reporters. He answered questions about the
case, dodging specifics. He also complained
about their pursuit of Jeanne and Jan Rifkin.

"We know everyone has a job to do, but
there reaches a point when we're walking to
the courtroom and a seventy-one-year-old
woman should not be physically shoved, a
microphone physically put on her face, and
be shouted at," he said. "These people are not
targets of any criminal proceedings. They
just happen to be, by quirk of birth, related
to a person who is a defendant in a case.

They should not be treated so unprofession-ally."

That said, he went on to lambaste the state troopers for their interrogation of his client.

"I'm shocked they didn't see fit to videotape his statement," he said. "It's standard proce-dure in any high-visibility case. On video we can actually hear the words and see the de-meanor and maybe the mental state of the person. I'm shocked and I'm surprised that it wasn't done. It leaves unanswered ques-tions. Why wasn't it done? Why weren't nor-mal procedures followed?"

Sale made it clear that he fully intended to raise this issue in future court hearings. It might turn out, he added, that none of Joel Rifkin's conversation with police would be admissible in court. His client's constitu-tional rights, after all, must be protected.

"By using the argument that they found the bodies where Joel Rifkin said, therefore he must have done it—that's begging the question," Sale said. "The question is whether they did the right thing or not. We don't have to explain why they found the bodies. They have to prove that there is a connection and that my client is responsible for them being there."

Over at state trooper headquarters, the cops were talking too. Captain Walter Heesch called an afternoon press conference to present an update on the case. But within minutes he was busy fielding questions about the lack of a videotaped confession. Heesch skillfully dismissed the implied criticism.

"Based on the timing and the available things at the time, we just didn't do it," he said.

"Isn't that going to hurt your case?" he was asked.

Heesch hesitated only a moment.

"I don't know," he said. "Next question?"

The captain was clearly wary of the press. He gave them laconic answers, often vague. His refusal to answer specific queries frustrated reporters, but Heesch didn't care. It was more important, he knew, to stay focused on the investigation. Disclosing too much information could destroy a case. He'd seen it happen before.

So Heesch tried not to stray from his prepared remarks. He told reporters that the state police superintendent had temporarily transferred an additional fifteen detectives to help with the investigation, bringing the total number to fifty. He added that Lieutenant Ed Grant, an expert in serial killers, had been asked to work on the Rifkin case. Grant had been instrumental in developing a profile of Arthur Shawcross, the Rochester serial killer.

Cops were using two computer systems to help match victims: HALT, New York's Homicide Assessment Lead Tracking service, and Vi-CAP, the FBI's Violent Criminal Apprehension Program.

Later that day more than twenty-five investigators from a variety of law enforcement agencies were meeting to pool data. "As you probably realize, there are a number of unsolved homicides," he said. "We want to see if any of them are connected with Joel Rifkin."

When pressed, Heesch answered a few questions about Rifkin's conversation with Capers and Louder.

Rifkin, he said, was more specific on some of the murders than others. The investigators did not believe he'd held any of his victims prisoner.

But they definitely believed that Rifkin fit the profile of a serial killer—someone who kills four or more people with a cooling-off period in between.

Heesch reminded the press that the investigation was still in the early stages. Yesterday they had linked eight deaths to Rifkin. Today, they had linked five more. Clearly there was a long way to go.

"It's a voluminous investigation," Heesch said. "There are a lot of things to cover. We've done many homicides before where we have one victim. Now we have numerous. It's complicated because of the different jurisdictions involved. But it's clear what we have to do."

As reporters began to leave, one asked a final question.

"Captain, do you think Joel Rifkin wanted to get caught?"

Heesch didn't answer for a moment. Generally, he didn't like to speculate on a criminal's behavior.

But then he just shrugged.

"He's driving down the street with no plates on a vehicle. He's got a dead body in the car that's decomposed. Now, that's not meticulous," he said.

Chapter 12

AS police released names of Joel Rifkin's victims, bands of journalists raced to interview family members. One of the first they found was María Alonso. By late afternoon, shortly after Rifkin was arraigned, a line snaked outside her Brooklyn apartment. Everyone wanted to know how María Alonso felt. What did she think about Joel Rifkin? What would she do to him if she could?

"I always thought that I was going to be so happy once I knew what happened to my daughter," she told reporters. "I'd get my life back. But it's worse than the beginning—to know that that man killed my daughter. I see his face and I can't get to him."

Reporters asked her how she'd feel if Joel Rifkin pleaded insane. María Alonso's voice grew bitter.

"He's not insane," she said. "If he remembers where he threw my daughter's body thirteen months before and the details of all these girls, where he threw them, nobody in the world can convince me that that guy is insane. He's just plain evil. That's how he got his kicks. That's how he felt powerful: killing innocent, defenseless women. Because otherwise he's nothing, he's a nobody. He's not good at anything. He's a sadist personality."

She told reporters how she had tried to tell police about her daughter's disappearance. She told them about the officer who said Annie had probably met someone and gone to the Bahamas.

"If they would have listened to me, maybe a few lives could have been saved," she said. "But they didn't care. They don't care for drug addicts. They really don't. How many girls did that monster kill after he killed my daughter?"

And then María spoke for the other mothers who would learn the fate of their children. Her words were quoted on the front pages of the newspapers and broadcast on the evening news.

"He did not kill seventeen prostitutes—he killed seventeen daughters," she said evenly. "Some of them were mothers. They have sisters and brothers. And they left a lot of people behind suffering and missing them. There is a story behind every one of them."

María paused to wipe away her tears. "When I see one of these girls in the street, I do not look at them with disgust. I look at them with pity. They're still people. My daughter had to sell her body to support her drug habit. I'm not naive. When you have a drug addiction, whatever money you make working is not enough. If you are into crack, you do what you do. I never saw my daughter doing drugs or selling her body, but I knew she did it. But my daughter was not born a prostitute. Only drugs made her a prostitute."

Over the next few days police fended off criticism. Why had no one linked the murders of more than a dozen young prostitutes over the past two years? Were women who sold their bodies unsympathetic victims? Did their deaths somehow mean less? In their defense, police said that no one had reported these women missing. "Prostitutes are out on the street at all hours," said New York City Police Commissioner Raymond Kelly. "There aren't going to be any witnesses. . . . This is a big city. We have a lot of missing person's reports. And also, if you're reporting someone missing you may not necessarily identify them as a prostitute."

Various experts on serial killers spoke out as well. They explained that prostitutes were easy prey because most had no connections—no family or friends who'd even notice if they were gone. "There are a lot of people in this world who don't have a connection to their families," said Colonel Wayne Bennett, head of the New York State Police Bureau of Criminal Investigation.

But that wasn't the case with Joel Rifkin's victims. They had families. They had people who cared. In fact, many relatives of the missing women attempted to file reports with police. In New York, however, a missing person's report is taken only if the person is under eighteen or over sixty-five, or has a medical problem or history of mental illness.

Besides, as Assistant District Attorney Fred Klein pointed out, no one would ever know how these women encountered Joel Rifkin. No one could say what really happened. "Not all of the victims have a record of prostitution or any proof that they were prostitutes," he said. "He says they're prostitutes. Unfortunately, the victims can't tell us their side."

One wonders what Leah Evens would say. She was twenty-eight years old and a mother of two when she was murdered by Joel Rifkin. It was a Saturday night. Her children, Julian, five, and Eve, three, were home, sleeping. They lived with Leah's mother in a Park Slope, Brooklyn, town house.

The mystery of what had happened to Leah Evens ended when police found her driver's license and employee identification card in Rifkin's bedroom. For months before, no one knew where she was. Her corpse lay in Potter's Field, a dumping ground for unclaimed bodies.

Leah grew up in an ambitious family. Her mother, Susan, worked in the public relations office of Cooper Union; her father, Lester, was a Manhattan Civil Court judge.

She was close to her parents, particularly her dad. In 1985, when her father became embroiled in a very public—and humiliating—scandal, Leah suffered along with him.

She was away at school, attending Sarah Lawrence College. She read about her father's disgrace every morning in the newspapers. It started out innocently. Her father, then sixty-one, was sitting at his bench one morning in Arraignment Part II at 100 Centre Street and watched as cops led a group of prostitutes into the room. Among them was Beth Reilly, a pretty eighteen-year-old. Reilly had been arrested a week earlier and fined a hundred dollars. She paid half, and promised to return with the rest.

She never did. Police rearrested Beth Reilly. She sat waiting in Lester Evens's courtroom for a friend to post bail. She leaned back on the bench and yawned. Loudly.

Lester Evens grinned. He motioned to Beth Reilly, inviting her to join him on the bench. Giggling, she did.

Beth Reilly spent the morning sitting with the judge. Then he told her she was released.

"Go home," Evens said, smiling. "Call it time served."

Judge Lester Evens was branded a fool and a dirty old man. His colleagues nicknamed him Judge Hooker. He was eventually censured for "undignified behavior" by state officials. His wife eventually left him and moved to Park Slope.

Two years later, Judge Evens was defeated in a primary.

It was a difficult time for Leah Evens. Her father's public humiliation was crushing. But she remained close to him—she didn't care what anyone else said. Besides, by the time her father had lost his reelection, she had enough troubles of her own.

By then, Leah Evens had left Sarah Lawrence and was having problems finding a job. She eventually began working as a waitress and cook in a restaurant on Seventh Ave in Manhattan. For a time, she had a boyfriend. They had two children together—Julian and Eve.

Then Leah's boyfriend left her.

Despondent, Leah Evens turned to drugs. She began to work the streets of Twelfth Street and Second Avenue to pay for her daily fix. On at least one occasion, she was arrested for prostitution.

Yet once or twice a week Leah Evens still visited her dad at his opulent Manhattan apartment. Back home at her mother's town house in Brooklyn, Leah often sat on the stoop outside watching her children play.

Somehow, Leah Evens managed to hide the worst of her disease from the people she loved the most.

On February 27, 1993, she could no longer protect them. Or herself.

Joel Rifkin says that on that night he offered Leah Evens forty dollars for sex in his pickup. He says the judge's daughter agreed. When it was over, he strangled her.

Joel Rifkin then drove east, Leah's body still in the pickup with him. He passed the exit for East Meadow and kept going. He went about fifty miles farther and then turned down County Road 51. It was before dawn. The road was deserted.

A few miles later he turned on a gravel road, Old Riverhead–Moriches Road. Rifkin didn't know it, but he'd entered the 192-acre Hidden Hill Farm in Speonk, in the hamlet of Northampton. The owner rented lots to several Korean farmers who grew mostly wild vegetables and herbs. Several dogs roamed the area, keeping trespassers away.

But Rifkin stayed at the edge of the farm, away from the dogs and the trailers where the farmers lived. He stopped the pickup just a hundred yards from the road. Then he dragged the body of Julian and Eve's mother through the woods another hundred yards. He dug a shallow grave and dumped the body inside. He covered it with dirt.

For the next two and a half months the body of Leah Evens lay unnoticed.

It was May 9—Mother's Day. Early in the morning, five Koreans from Queens were out hunting for wild vegetables. They'd gotten permission from one of the farmers on the land.

They traipsed through the woods, searching for edible ferns. Then one of the group members spied a cluster of them. He reached down. He gasped. Amid the bushes was a hand sticking straight up.

The group drove into the town of Speonk and called the police. When cops arrived, they cordoned off the area and examined the body.

It was badly decomposed—almost a skeleton. Bits of red or orange nail polish still clung to the nails. The next day police put out her description. She was white, at least twenty years old, with dark brown hair at least shoulder length. She weighed ninety-five pounds and was tiny—four foot nine. She wore a long-sleeved white pullover shirt with a Gap label, and a blue button-front sweater.

The Southampton Town Police Department, which handles the area, tried to interest the local media in the story about the body. At first reporters declined. At the time, the hot story in Long Island's East End was a man who was torturing and killing animals in Sag Harbor.

But later, the *Hampton Chronicle News* ran a front-page article: POLICE SEEK TO IDENTIFY BODY DISCOVERED IN NORTHAMPTON, the headline read.

The article quoted the Suffolk County medical examiner, Stuart Dawson, who said that autopsy results were inconclusive and that they revealed no obvious cause of death. That, Dawson added, didn't rule out foul play.

Over the next few weeks, Suffolk County homicide police worked on a computer-enhanced composite of what the dead woman might have looked like. They had just completed it when Rifkin was caught and told detectives about Leah Evens.

During his interrogation with Capers and Louder, Rifkin described Evens, detailing where they met and how he'd disposed of the body. But the East Meadow man had trouble remembering her name. Capers and Louder waited. Rifkin thought some more. Then he shook his head.

"I can't remember," he said. But then Rifkin recalled something else. "I kept some stuff from her," he told them.

Indeed he had. With the driver's license and employee ID card found in Rifkin's bedroom, detectives connected Leah Evens's name with the body found in Speonk. They were then able to contact Lester and Susan Evens.

And so Leah Evens's parents got the news they had prayed they would never hear. Over the next few weeks they managed to evade the media; neither spoke publicly about their daughter. But privately, Susan and Lester Evens grieved for their Leah. Somehow they found the strength to do the unthinkable— to explain to their little grandchildren why their mother never came home last winter, and never would again.

Not only did Joel Rifkin forget Mary Catherine Williams's name, he couldn't remember that he had murdered her. She was the one victim that Joel Rifkin never mentioned. Police believe he may have simply lost count. He told them seventeen; police think the actual number was eighteen. Joel Rifkin may have forgotten that he strangled Mary Catherine Williams.

Her family never will. Catherine, as they called her, was petite and dark haired. She was a talented gymnast and dancer and dreamed of becoming an actress. She had a series of bit parts in movies produced by a North Carolina film company.

Catherine earned a bachelor of fine arts degree from the University of North Carolina at Chapel Hill and had been a homecoming queen and varsity cheerleader. When she graduated, she married Jay Cave, a football star from Charlotte.

The marriage ended in 1987. A few years later, Catherine moved to New York to pursue her acting dream. But acting jobs were tough to find in the city. Catherine took a job at an advertising agency and began to wonder if she would ever make it as an actress.

Back home in Charlotte she'd used cocaine a few times. In New York, she began to use it more. Then one day she realized she couldn't stop. When she ran out of money for drugs, she became a prostitute.

For a time, it seemed there was hope. About

eight months before she died, Catherine met a thirty-six-year-old Japanese businessman and fell in love. At the time, she was living in a crack house in the East Village.

Her boyfriend encouraged her to get into a program. Catherine said she would. She went home to Charlotte for Christmas. Her parents knew about her drug problem and begged her to stay. They would help, they insisted.

But Catherine was adamant. She returned to New York, insisting she could handle it.

She couldn't. Her cocaine use continued. Then, in October 1992, Catherine and her boyfriend had a fight over her drug use. He dropped her off at the crack house. He never saw her again.

A few nights later Catherine met Joel Rifkin. He had just taken a new job. He had signed up with Dunhill Temporary Systems, a local agency that assigned its clients to various jobs with large companies. Rifkin was placed at Olympus America in Woodbury. Every day he joined an assembly line of ten to fifteen workers at a large table. He cleaned and repaired cameras. Sometimes he worked alone, packing and loading cameras.

At night he drove into Manhattan. At some point he noticed the pretty dark-haired girl on the street, the former cheerleader from North Carolina.

Two months later, just before Christmas, Mary Catherine's naked, badly decomposed body was found in a wooded area of Yorktown, in Westchester. A medical examiner found cocaine in her system. As with Leah Evens, as with Anna Lopez, as with so many others, no one knew who she was. Her body lay unclaimed in Potter's Field until the following summer.

That's when her credit cards were found in Joel Rifkin's home. Police called Catherine's parents in Charlotte. Her father, Egbert, a dentist, sent his daughter's records to New York. Police made a positive identification.

Police called the Williamses with the tragic news on the same day that their younger daughter, Susan, got engaged.

"When something good happens, something horrible happens too," Doris Williams said, breaking into sobs.

About a month after he strangled Mary Catherine Williams, Joel Rifkin encountered his next victim. Her name was Jenny Soto.

Chapter 13

THE last time Jessy Olmedo saw her sister Jenny it was 11:00 P.M. on November 16, 1992.

They had spent the evening hanging out in Bushwick, Brooklyn, with Jenny's boyfriend, Popcorn. As usual, Jenny and Popcorn wound up in an argument. It was over something silly—it typically was. Jenny, twenty-three, had a quick temper. She grabbed a Goya bean can and threw it at Popcorn. Then she stormed out of the apartment.

Jessy followed her sister. She'd seen Jenny and Popcorn fight lots of times. But she knew that the couple adored each other. "Pop changed my life," Jenny always said. "He's the best thing that ever happened to me."

The sisters talked on the stoop. Their conversation turned to Jessy's pregnancy. She was due in four months. Jessy was just fifteen, nervous and a little scared. But Jenny was excited. She assured Jessy that everything was going to work out great. Jenny said she'd go back to school, get her GED, and land a good job. She'd rent an apartment, and Jessy and the baby would live with her. Jenny kept telling Jessy not to worry: she would always take care of her little sister.

On the sidewalk outside of Pop's apartment, Jenny's beeper went off. She looked down.

"It's Albert," she said. Albert was her ex-boyfriend. Recently, he'd been paroled from prison and was unhappy that Jenny was dating Popcorn. Albert had been calling a lot lately, begging for another chance.

It was getting late. Jessy was supposed to have been home by ten. The sisters walked to the subway and took the M train to Delancey Street in lower Manhattan. They crossed the platform. In a few minutes the F train approached. It was just a few stops to Park Slope, Brooklyn. The doors opened.

Suddenly Jenny stepped back.

"You go on ahead," she told Jessy. "I'm going to meet my friend."

"But Jenny—" Jessy began to say.

"Hurry up or you'll miss the train," Jenny said quickly, giving her sister a hug. "Don't worry. I'll be home by twelve-thirty."

Jessy stepped inside the car and the subway doors shut. At night, when she lies in bed, the house silent, Jessy can still picture Jenny standing on the platform as the train pulled out, waving goodbye.

Jenny Soto grew up in Brooklyn. Her mother, Margarita, had three children with her first husband. Then she met Jenny's father. Jenny never knew him. He was stabbed to death in a subway station on DeKalb Avenue a few months before she was born. Police never found his killer.

A few years later Margarita Gonzalez married Felix Olmedo. He worked in a shipyard in New Jersey. The couple had three children—Jessy, Charlie, and Eric. Felix was a good stepfather to Jenny; he raised her as one of his own children.

When Jenny was twelve, the family moved to a three-story brownstone on Thirteenth

Street in Park Slope, Brooklyn. Several of Margarita Gonzalez's siblings lived nearby. The families were close; they gathered for big Sunday dinners and celebrated birthdays and holidays together. Jenny spent a lot of time with her cousins.

But she was closest to her younger sister and brothers. Jenny was eight when Jessy was born. She played dolls with the little girl and fixed her hair in fancy braids. Jenny liked to pretend to be a teacher; Jessy was her student. She told her stories and taught her to dance.

When Charlie came along, Jenny doted on him too. As he grew older, she play-wrestled with him and took him to movies. Sometimes they watched soap operas together—*All My Children* was Jenny's favorite.

As for Eric, Jenny practically raised him. She showered him with hugs and kisses and wanted to give him anything he asked for. Two years before she died, Jenny brought home four yellow parakeets. When she saw how much Eric liked them, she gave them to him. Little Eric and his cousin Matthew named the birds Sito, Yiya, Christmas, and Yellow.

Jenny often took her three younger siblings along when she went shopping or to hang out with friends. As Jessy, Charlie, and Eric grew up, she warned them about smoking and drugs.

"Don't drink beer because after that, you'll go on to smoke pot, and keep continuing," she'd say. "Just don't try anything."

Sadly, she didn't follow her own advice. When Jenny was thirteen, she met Albert, a twenty-year-old from the neighborhood. Jenny's family believes that Albert was a bad influence. He used drugs. Before long, Jenny did too.

Jenny and Albert dated for seven years. At the end of eleventh grade, Jenny dropped out of John Jay High School. She went dancing in clubs almost every night, sometimes getting home after dawn.

Drugs took over. Desperate for money, Jenny turned to the streets. She was arrested several times—once for prostitution. Her fingerprints were placed on file at state police headquarters in Albany.

Despite her wild ways, Jenny remained close to her family. She still talked regularly about her goals. She wanted to be a dancer or a model. Almost every week, she bought film and asked friends to take her picture.

She turned to her little sister, Jessy, for updates on fashion.

Sometimes Jessy teased her. "You're getting old," she'd say. "You don't know the style."

Jenny always took Jessy's advice. She wore lots of gold jewelry and enormous gold earrings. She even bought $250 gold caps for her teeth.

"It's the style," Jessy would tell her. And Jenny would follow it.

Jenny loved to fix hair and makeup. She practiced on her sisters, cousins, and friends. Sometimes, before a party or for a special occasion, she styled her mother's hair. Margarita Gonzalez was proud of Jenny's talent. She encouraged her to become a professional hairstylist.

"Why don't you take that up?" Margarita Gonzalez would say. "You do it better than people who have a diploma."

Jenny always promised to think about it. "Ma, maybe I'll take that, but I don't know," she'd say. "There are so many things I want to do."

After Albert was arrested and sent to prison, Jenny met Popcorn. It was January 1992.

Jenny had gone with Jessy to visit Jessy's boyfriend. Popcorn was his best friend. At the time, Jenny was twenty-two; Popcorn was nineteen.

The young man noticed Jenny at once.

"Who's that girl?" Popcorn asked Jessy in a whisper. "I like her."

Jessy introduced her sister. The couple began to talk. Popcorn told Jenny that his real name was Noel—Pop was his rap name. He told her about his group. Someday he hoped to make it big.

Before long, Jenny and Popcorn were in love. She began to stay with him in the basement apartment he shared with his grandparents in Bushwick. Always, though, Jenny called home three or four times a day.

Bushwick wasn't too far from Park Slope, so Jenny went back and forth between Popcorn's place and her parents' home. She quickly discovered a fast route to Popcorn's—she took the F train into Manhattan and then the M train back to Brooklyn.

Her family noticed a change in Jenny. She began to talk about going back to school and getting her GED. Popcorn wanted her to, she said. Jenny talked a lot about the rap group.

Popcorn said she could be the group's producer.

In fact, the summer before she died, Jenny made the rounds, going to various clubs and trying to convince owners to audition the group. She even managed to get her little brother, Eric, involved. He introduced the act, and danced.

Jenny never missed rehearsals. They were held at the Playground, a Manhattan club. Sometimes she offered suggestions. Mostly, though, she just cheered them on. She was so proud of little Eric and Popcorn. At the end of each rehearsal she always applauded loudly.

At last it seemed as if Jenny Soto's life had turned around. She had new ambitions and a boyfriend she loved, one who didn't do drugs and who wanted her, too, to stay clean.

When Albert was paroled from jail and returned to Brooklyn, Jenny refused to see him. "No way will I go back to him," she told Jessy. "I love Pop."

Jessy was glad. She liked Popcorn. He was good for her sister. By then, Jessy was pregnant. As always, Jenny was there for her. It made Jessy feel safe, and reassured. Jenny was going to take care of everything.

Over the years, Jenny had often wondered aloud if she would ever be a parent. When she was dating Albert, she had become pregnant several times. Each time she'd had a miscarriage.

"I don't think I can ever have kids," Jenny told Jessy. "You have the baby. Don't worry about anything. We'll live together and I'll take care of the baby while you finish school."

It was her dream—to help raise her sister's child, to get an apartment of her own, to produce her boyfriend's rap group. Someday she would marry Popcorn. They'd already planned the wedding.

Joel Rifkin would destroy the dream.

Oddly, the summer before she was killed, Jenny Soto talked a lot about dying. She bought an ID card, and carried it in her wallet. She said that way if something happened to her, she could be identified.

One day she gave her gold chains to her mother.

"If I die," she said, "put them on me. I want my gold jewelry. And don't go putting me in a dress."

Margarita Gonzalez dismissed such morbid talk.

"What are you saying, Jenny?" she asked. "Don't talk that way."

The weekend before she was murdered, Jenny Soto went to her cousin Patricia's birthday party. Normally upbeat and chatty, Jenny seemed distant, detached. Her relatives suspected something was wrong but Jenny brushed off their concerns with a laugh. She was fine, she told them. Everything was fine.

No one was surprised that Jenny didn't express her real feelings. All her life she'd listened to their problems and doled out advice. But when it came to sharing her troubles, Jenny Soto was always silent. There was a part of Jenny Soto, her relatives knew, that no one could touch.

By that point, Jenny's family believed her drug problem was in the past. Over the summer Jenny attended a few Narcotics Anonymous meetings with a friend. But she didn't stay with the program. And her battle to stay clean raged within her.

Her preoccupation with death just before

she was killed haunts her family. They wonder what she knew.

Perhaps Jenny Soto sensed her drug problem might eventually bring her to a point where no one could save her. Perhaps she knew that by putting her life in danger, someday she'd find her luck running out.

It did.

On the night of November 16, 1992, drugs set the deadly chain of events in motion. When Jenny Soto left the subway station, police believe she went looking for cocaine. She found it. A medical examiner reported that traces of the drug were found in her body.

But at one point that night, Jenny stopped at a pay phone and called her mother. It was 11:45 P.M.

"Did Jessy get home all right?" Jenny asked.

Jessy was fine, but Margarita Gonzalez was angry. Jessy had come home way past her curfew.

Jenny tried to make peace.

"Don't be mad at Jessy," she said. "She was with me."

Margarita Gonzalez sighed. "And when are you coming home?" she asked.

"In an hour."

What happened next?

It is likely that Jenny Soto needed drug money. She may then have spotted the pickup truck, as it slowly cruised the streets of lower Manhattan.

Chapter 14

OF all the women Joel Rifkin killed, Jenny Soto fought for life the hardest. She kicked and scratched. She dug her nails into his face. When a coroner examined the body, all of Jenny's nails had been broken. Bits of Rifkin's skin were buried underneath.

During his interrogation, Rifkin mentioned Jenny by name several times. He remembered her well. She'd taken a long time to die. Finally, he'd had to snap her neck.

When Jenny never showed at her parents' house, her family was not overly concerned. Jessy had explained that Jenny's ex-boyfriend, Albert, had beeped her. Jenny must have gone to see him.

The family decided that Jenny was probably worried that her mother would be angry. Jenny knew Margarita Gonzalez wasn't crazy about Albert. Jenny's boyfriend, Popcorn, would also be upset. Jenny had probably decided to wait a little while until things settled down. Then she'd come home. She always did.

Police believe Jenny Soto was killed at about 2:00 A.M., a little more than two hours after she called home to see that Jessy was safe. Joel Rifkin told investigators that after he killed Jenny Soto he drove up the East River Drive into the Bronx. He pulled over at the side and dragged Jenny's body from the truck. At the edge of a rocky hill, he dropped it.

The body tumbled down the hill, landing at the edge of the Harlem River, at the foot of Lincoln Avenue. It was discovered at 8:00 A.M. wearing only a red and orange striped shirt, pushed up. Jenny's large gold shell earrings and her wallet, filled with pictures of Popcorn, were missing.

In the days following Jenny's disappearance, Jessy frequently called her sister's beeper. She punched in their home phone number, and then her special code: 13. Jessy couldn't understand why Jenny wasn't calling back.

She's with Albert, and she doesn't want Mom to know, Jessy kept thinking. But it's so weird. She always calls me back.

Jessy decided to wait for Thanksgiving. Jenny never missed a family gathering. Surely she would be there. If not, at least she'd call.

On Thanksgiving, Jenny's family ate in silence. When the dishes were done and leftovers put away, Jessy turned to her mother.

"I have a bad feeling, Mom," Jessy told her mother. "I've been beeping her and she doesn't call me back. Popcorn's been beeping her too. It doesn't make sense. I'm her little sister. I'm her best friend. Why wouldn't she call back? And Popcorn. If she loves him, why wouldn't she call?"

Margarita Gonzalez tried to dismiss the nagging fear that was growing inside her too.

"We'll see," was all she said. "We'll wait and see."

On December 1 Margarita Gonzalez decided she'd waited long enough. She told her daughters, Margie and Jessy, that she was planning to go to the police station that day and report Jenny missing.

She never got the chance. By midmorning, a police car had pulled up to the house. In the weeks since Jenny's body was discovered, police had checked fingerprints against thousands on file in the computer. Jenny's prints were on file because of her prior arrest for prostitution. When they matched, a team of detectives showed up at Margarita Gonzalez's town house.

Margie answered the knock at the door.

"Does Jenny Soto live here?" the detective asked.

Margie said she did. She told the detectives that her sister had been missing for several weeks. As she spoke, her mother slowly walked into the hall.

The detective looked at Margarita Gonzalez. "Are you her mother?" he asked.

Margarita nodded. She motioned to the men to come inside. They all stood, awkwardly, in the living room.

"We found a body with a tattoo on her right hip," the detective said.

Margie took a deep breath. "My sister had a tattoo," she said slowly.

"It says 'Albert' on it, with a little heart."

Margarita Gonzalez broke down. She began to weep hysterically.

The detectives told her to try to be calm; they couldn't be 100 percent positive the body they found was her daughter's. "It does fit the description," one said gently. "But someone has to go to the medical examiner's office and identify the body."

"What's going on?" a voice rang out from the hallway. It was Jessy. She'd been visiting her cousin down the block. Her uncle had noticed the police car and told her to hurry home. "Jessy," he'd said. "There are cops at your house."

Jessy didn't hesitate. She ran home and rushed into the living room. She pushed past the detectives and dropped to her knees beside her mother, sitting on the couch, rocking. Margarita Gonzalez was sobbing.

"What's going on? What's going on?" Jessy kept saying.

"Oh, my God," her mother wept. "I think Jenny's dead."

* * *

185

The next day, Margie and two cousins, Magdalia and Jerry, went to Bellevue Hospital in Manhattan to identify Jenny's body. Margarita Gonzalez was too distraught to go. Jessy was by now six months pregnant. She, too, stayed home.

When the others saw the body they barely recognized Jenny. Her face was blue, her lips and nose swollen, her mouth agape. Black marks covered her neck.

The medical examiner told Margie Gonzalez that cocaine was found in Jenny's system. He said that she had been strangled, but not beaten—the body appeared that way because it had been thrown down a rocky hill.

The broken nails, he explained, were because Jenny had savagely fought her attacker.

In the months that followed, Jenny's family tried to find out what happened the night she was killed. At first, their suspicions turned to Albert. A week before Jenny was strangled he'd shown up at the house, trying to cajole her into going back to him. Jenny was resolute. She loved Popcorn. She wouldn't leave him. Not ever.

They quarreled, and Albert stormed out of

the house. Jenny's family recalled his parting words: "If you ain't going to be with me, you ain't going to be with anyone else," he'd shouted.

Detectives spoke to Albert. But his alibi was solid. Besides, Albert had never been violent with Jenny in the past.

At the funeral, he wept uncontrollably. He leaned over the casket, kissing Jenny's hands and face. Her mother had dressed her in a turtleneck, to hide the marks on her neck.

Margarita Gonzalez pushed Albert aside. "Stop kissing her," she snapped. "If you had loved her, you wouldn't have fought with her the way you did. I think you killed my daughter."

Albert shook his head, crying. "I loved her," he kept saying. "I loved her."

"You threatened her," Margarita Gonzalez said. "If you did it, I'm going to find out. And you're going to pay."

In time, though, Jenny's family was less convinced that Albert was the killer. He seemed truly distraught over Jenny's death. He dropped by the house frequently, wanting to talk about her.

"If you ever find out who did it," he always said, "tell me. I'll kill him."

Maybe Albert wasn't her daughter's killer, Margarita Gonzalez thought. But then who was?

The family became wary of Jenny's friends. They even wondered about Popcorn. Sometimes, Jessy acted cold to him when he stopped by to visit.

"What's the matter with you?" he'd say.

"Nothing, just leave," Jessy would snap.

Later she often felt badly about the way she'd acted. She'd always liked Popcorn. But her mother kept reminding her that anyone could be Jenny's killer. "We can't trust anybody," Margarita Gonzalez would say. And Jessy would nod silently.

The family didn't feel the police took Jenny's murder seriously. Two days after the body was identified, one of the detectives assigned to the case went on vacation. In the weeks that followed, Margie Gonzalez called the precinct frequently, asking if there was any news. Detectives never took the calls. She left messages. No one ever called back.

"They think she was a prostitute, and they don't care," Jessy told her sister bitterly.

"Even if she was, that has nothing to do with it."

Finally, Margie and a cousin, Alma, took the subway to the Bronx. They went to the police station and asked for the homicide detectives. At first, the officer on duty said no one was available to speak to them. Then Alma pulled out a badge. She, too, was a cop.

At last Margie met with the detectives handling Jenny's murder. They told her that Jenny might have been killed by a serial killer because police had found several other bodies of women dumped in area waters. But so far they had nothing new to report. But, they assured her, the death of Jenny Soto was an ongoing investigation.

On March 21, 1993, Jessy gave birth to a boy. At first she thought of naming him John. That was pretty close to Jenny. But her family didn't like the name. Someone suggested Jeremiah. Jessy liked it. She thought Jenny would have too.

When she rocked her baby, Jessy often thought of all the old plans. Jenny was going to be there. Jenny had always been there for her.

Once, not long after Jenny's funeral, Jessy

called her sister's old beeper number. She
punched in her home number and waited.
She wanted to know who, if anyone, had
Jenny's beeper. She wanted to ask how the
person had gotten it.

Within minutes, a woman with a thick
Asian accent called back.

"Who's this?" the woman asked.

"Who's this?" Jessy answered.

The woman hung up. When Jessy beeped
again, the woman did not return the call.

Not knowing who killed Jenny Soto tore her
family apart. For months, Margarita Gonzalez had been going to church daily, lighting
candles and praying for strength.

In May, she prayed for an answer.

She went to church and lit candles to the
Virgin Mary and St. Anthony. Then she
went to her daughter's grave. She arranged
flowers atop the gravestone. She got on her
knees and touched the ground gently.

In the stillness of the cemetery, through
her tears, Margarita Gonzalez spoke to her
daughter. "Let it be for your birthday or my
birthday that I find out who did this," she
said aloud. Jenny's twenty-fourth birthday

would have been June 6. Margarita's fiftieth was July 1.

On June 29, a few minutes past noon, the phone rang. It was Margarita's sister.

"Put on the news," she said. "Some man was strangling girls. Maybe he's the one who killed Jenny."

Margarita switched the channel. She watched the report. She saw Joel Rifkin as he emerged from state police headquarters in the white jumpsuit. Then she called her daughter Margie.

"Did you see the news?" she asked.

Margie said she had. In the background, Margie's four-year-old son, Matthew, was yelling.

"He's the killer, Mommy," the little boy kept repeating, pointing to the television. "That man killed Jenny. I know he's the one. Mommy, he killed Jenny."

After Margarita hung up she lay down on the couch and thought about Jenny. She wondered about this man, this Joel Rifkin. How could he have killed so many young girls? Could Jenny be one of his victims?

The phone rang. Jessy stepped into the kitchen and picked it up. She had been upstairs taking care of Jeremiah and hadn't seen the news. She had never heard of Joel Rifkin.

"Is Jenny Soto at home?" a man asked.

Jessy tightened. "Why are you calling for Jenny Soto?" she asked sharply. "She passed away."

"This is Investigator Patrick Caffrey of the New York State Police," he said. "We are investigating the serial killer Joel Rifkin."

"Joel Rifkin?"

"Do you mind if I ask you how Jenny Soto was killed?"

"She got strangled."

"We called because Joel Rifkin mentioned the last name Soto."

In the next room, Margarita Gonzalez couldn't understand what was going on. Something about Jenny. Something about her killer. Margarita panicked. She began yelling at Jessy to hang up. "It could be the killer trying to get information!" she screamed.

Jessy tried to calm her mother. She covered the receiver with her hand.

"It's the police," she said. She asked the detective if he wanted to talk to Jenny Soto's mother. Jessy explained that her mother did not understand English fluently. The detective said that wasn't a problem—they would supply a translator.

In Spanish, the translator told Margarita Gonzalez about Joel Rifkin. He said that during his conversation with police Rifkin had described Jenny's tattoo. Later, investigators had found Jenny's wallet and jewelry in his bedroom. He asked if the family could identify Jenny's earrings. Margarita said they could. She hung up the phone and began to sob uncontrollably.

By the end of the day, reporters filled Margarita Gonzalez's living room. Most of the journalists had already been to María Alonso's apartment a few miles away.

Margarita Gonzalez tried to talk about her daughter, to express her feelings about Joel Rifkin. But she was distraught. The pressure was too much.

Jessy took over. Holding Jeremiah, she talked about Jenny and how the family was coping with the news. "It's a relief to know that they caught my sister's killer," she said, "but it still hurts because we were getting over it and now all the feelings are back. I still feel like she's going to come home. I can't believe she's gone. She was a great big part of my life."

Two days later, Margarita Gonzalez turned fifty. She cried all day. But she thought about her prayer—how she had pleaded with God to give her an answer. And He had. Just when she'd asked for it—between her daughter's birthday and her own.

That night, Jessy put her arms around her mother. "God must have seen that you are a good lady and that Jenny didn't deserve this," she said. "He answered your prayer."

Chapter 15

EVERY day, investigators gathered at the command center in a large conference room at state police headquarters in East Farmingdale. On the walls were maps of the region, as well as a list of the victims. Bits of evidence—jewelry, credit cards, clothing— lay strewn on tables.

The detectives' job was prodigious. Complicating matters was the fact that there were many different jurisdictions and law enforcement agencies involved. For the state police, it was important not to slight other agencies. Deciding who had jurisdiction was an important political task.

Within days of Rifkin's arrest, police located the body of Iris Sanchez under the mattress at JFK Airport, and an unidentified woman in the dense pine barrens off Route 31 in Westhampton. The skeletal remains had been buried beneath heavy underbrush in the woods near a power line tower.

Cops identified Tiffany Bresciani, the woman in the back of the pickup. They matched names with bodies they'd already found in the last two years—Anna Lopez, Mary Ellen DeLuca, Leah Evens, Lorraine Orvieto, Barbara Jacobs, Yun Lee, Mary Catherine Williams, and Jenny Soto.

They continued to work on the others— including locating the body of Julie Blackbird, a Texas native Rifkin had confessed to killing. She was thirty-one when she'd disappeared off the streets of lower Manhattan. She'd had a lengthy record of arrest, including two for drug possession and six for prostitution.

Police also wanted to find out about the three bodies Rifkin said he'd dismembered, and the still-unidentified woman in the third steel drum.

For several days, a dozen state police in Rockland County hunted for another victim believed to have been dumped in a wooded area about twenty miles north of New York City. Rifkin had given investigators copious directions; he even drew a map. He explained that he'd picked up the woman last fall and killed her. Then he'd dumped her body not far from the intersection of Routes 303 and 59 in West Nyack.

Police took four dogs along for the search. They turned up nothing.

State police also searched areas of the campus of the State University at Farmingale, where Rifkin had attended horticulture courses. They hunted at Kev's Landscaping and Design, where Rifkin had rented space for his trailer. During the interrogation, Rifkin had confessed to storing bodies there too.

Owner Kevin Seck wasn't surprised to see police at his door. Ever since he'd heard the news about Joel Rifkin, he'd been expecting them.

"I don't want any negative publicity," Seck said at once, even before the detectives spoke. "Is everything going to be kept quiet?"

Investigators assured him it would be. A few hours later, seven cops arrived with dogs. Seck unlocked the gate and showed them where Joel Rifkin had stored his equipment. Police thanked Seck for his cooperation. They didn't have a search warrant, but Seck told them it didn't matter. They were welcome to look around all they wanted.

"Just please," he reminded the cops, "let's keep this quiet."

Seck doesn't know who leaked the news—the police say the district attorney's office, and the DA blames the cops—but within a few hours hordes of reporters and film crews were at his gate. They snapped photos of the police and dogs digging and exploring. Finally, Seck escaped to his home. When he arrived, he found a *Newsday* reporter and photographer waiting on his front porch.

"No comment," the landscaper said curtly.

Seck's worst fears were realized. The next day the *New York Post* mistakenly ran a picture of Seck's other business—a shopping mall—with the tagline HOUSE OF HORRORS. The article went on to say that Joel Rifkin had stored bodies behind the mall.

Seck was irate. It was bad enough that his landscaping business was connected to Joel Rifkin. But now his shopping mall. . . .

He called a lawyer. "I'm going to sue those guys," he grumbled.

He thought of Spaceplex, the indoor amusement park in Nesconset, Long Island.

It had gotten a bad rap the year before when a Bay Shore man announced the child he had taken there had been kidnapped. It turned out that the man, John Esposito, had made up the story. In reality, he'd locked the ten-year-old girl, Katie Beers, in a dungeon he'd built beneath his garage.

Even after the truth came out, Spaceplex owners suffered a drop in business. Kevin Seck drove to work wondering if now his shopping mall would too.

He tried not to worry about it. Maybe no one would remember. Seck wanted to forget he'd ever heard the name Joel Rifkin.

He got out of his car and walked toward the mall.

"Hey, got any dead bodies in there?" a young man yelled out.

At 1492 Garden Street, crowds gathered daily. One of the first spectators to arrive on the scene was a young man named Seth Frankel. The teenager from Merrick, Long Island, had achieved some notoriety in the past year. Frankel lived down the block from Amy Fisher. When reporters and camera crews filled the streets outside his home, Seth Frankel managed to present himself as a good friend of Amy's. In fact, he told reporters earnestly, he'd even seen naked photographs of her.

None of that was true. Still, Frankel had schmoozed his way onto several talk shows. He was quoted in various newspapers and in a book about Fisher. When the fuss along Berkley Lane finally died down, Seth Frankel was disappointed.

So when the Joel Rifkin story broke, the young man grabbed a friend and headed to East Meadow. He wasn't going to miss the excitement.

Hanging out by the house, he was heard to say that he knew Joel Rifkin. Pretty well, in fact.

Reporters quickly spread the word to newcomers: Don't pay any attention to this kid.

Meanwhile, photographers camped out on the sidewalk were rapidly getting bored. Reporters had neighbors to interview; they had nothing to photograph. Jeanne and Jan Rifkin seldom ventured out of the house.

"Maybe Joey Buttafuoco will come over and offer consolation to the family," one photographer suggested hopefully.

Another glanced at his watch. "He better

not show up until two-thirty—when I'm on overtime," he said.

The first one yawned. This was not a plum assignment.

But the Rifkin stint quickly got interesting. A free-lance photographer decided to shoot the large pile of debris in the Rifkin driveway. Police had not yet removed it.

From across the street, Frank Barton was watching. His temper flared.

The tall, imposing man had lived in the neighborhood for more than a decade. He liked Jeanne Rifkin. Over the years they'd often talked about gardening. Barton, too, was a talented landscaper.

Since Joel Rifkin's arrest, Barton and his wife, Judy, had tried to help Jeanne and Jan however they could. They brought groceries and watered the Rifkins' garden. Barton told Jeanne Rifkin he'd try to keep the press from getting too close.

He took his promise seriously. When he spied the photographer stepping on the Rifkins' driveway and snapping photos, Frank Barton barreled across the street.

"Get off the property," he thundered. "What do you think you're doing? What are you taking pictures of anyway? It's garbage.

What are you doing taking pictures of garbage?"

The photographer glanced up for just a moment. She continued her work.

"The mother doesn't deserve this," Barton growled. He turned away.

"What about the victims?" the photographer said softly, to no one in particular.

A crowd of journalists watched the exchange silently. This was getting interesting. Frank Barton wasn't finished. He pointed to the film crew from Channel 7. A few of them were seated in folding chairs on the sidewalk.

"Is this a party over here?" Barton bellowed. "Do you mind removing the lounge chairs? This isn't a picnic."

The journalists exchanged glances. Barton continued to rage.

"This woman is suffering," he said loudly, motioning to the Rifkin house. "She didn't do anything. Neither did the sister. Leave the poor lady alone."

The photographers rolled their eyes as Barton stormed back into his house. They moved their chairs from the sidewalk to the street.

"Happy now?" one said to himself.

"Maybe he's an accomplice," another added.

Frank Barton watched from his living room window. Lounge chairs in the street, indeed.

"Wise guys," he muttered.

A few days later, Frank Barton emerged from his house again. He had another problem with the press—a big one. And this time everyone at the scene agreed he was right.

A TV cameraman had walked up the Rifkins' driveway into the backyard. Back turned, he'd urinated. Barton was watching from his living room window. He practically turned white.

He blasted out of the house and shouted at reporters.

"Look at your colleague," he yelled. "Why don't you take a picture of that? Why don't you put that in your newspaper? You're getting all the dirt. Why don't you print that?"

At that point, the cameraman returned to the sidewalk.

"I can't believe you did that," Barton shouted.

The man didn't seem chagrined.

"They won't let me go in the house," he

said, shrugging. "What am I supposed to do?"

"That's your problem," Barton snapped. "Next time, bring your own facilities."

Later, a few journalists approached Frank Barton and apologized for their colleague.

"We're not all like that," said Roger Stern from WNBC-TV.

Barton was slightly mollified.

"Some of you guys are okay," he conceded.

As the weeks passed, Frank Barton found a new enemy: the spectators. At least the reporters, he had to admit, were doing their job. But the constant flow of tourists to the corner of Garden Street and Spruce Lane was driving him crazy.

"Look at these people," he'd often say to his wife. "They stand and watch for hours. What are they looking at?"

Barton became pretty good at sending spectators off on a chase.

One Saturday, a group pulled up. A young man leaned out the car window.

"Do you know where Rafkin lives?"

"Who?" asked Barton, faking interest.

"Rafkin. Joe Rafkin."

"Don't know anyone by that name."

"You know, the killer."

"Oh," Frank Barton nodded enthusiastically. "Of course. He lives down there." He pointed. "About two blocks. Maybe three."

The man looked confused.

"No, no," he said. "I think he lives right around here."

"Sorry," Frank Barton said without a hint of a smile. "He lives down there."

"What they expect to see, I don't know," Barton later grumbled to his wife, Judy. "Look, here's another one. Looking at the wrong house. Oh. Now he gets it. Now he'll make a U-turn, come by, and stare. Genius."

For Frank Barton and others in East Meadow, the unfolding of Joel Rifkin's murderous deeds meant an ugly stain on their hometown. Everyone knew how Merrick and Massapequa, Long Island, had quickly become synonymous with Amy Fisher and Joey Buttafuoco. Residents in East Meadow were determined to ensure their town wouldn't be the same.

Ben Mevorach, news director of WGSM, a Long Island radio station, grew up in East Meadow and went to high school with Joel

Rifkin. He fought the urge to ignore the story.

"Part of me is very defensive," he said. "We don't want East Meadow to be smudged the way Amy Fisher smudged Merrick. But how can I walk away from covering a major story?"

He didn't. On the air, he offered his memories of Joel Rifkin and reported the various updates given by the state police. But Mevorach grew tired of the story, fast. His mother, Libby, did too. Once when she was out shopping she came home to a message on her answering machine. It was a salesman, calling from another state.

"Geez," the voice said. "I guess no one's home in East Meadow anymore. Ha-ha. Just kidding."

Libby Mevorach called her son at the radio station and told him about the message. "You might want to use this on the air," she said. "Although I don't find it funny."

Long Island's Jewish community, too, was sensitive about Joel Rifkin. Jewish residents were frequently heard noting that Joel Rifkin was actually adopted—he probably wasn't Jewish after all. It had been the same thing with David Berkowitz, the Son of Sam killer. He, too, was adopted.

Alan Whitlock, Rifkin's high school friend, even got a call from a reporter who worked for an Israeli newspaper.

"How do you feel that a fellow Jew is a serial killer?" the reporter asked.

Whitlock was stunned. He told the reporter that it meant nothing to him. Joel Rifkin's religion was completely irrelevant.

"Is that what you're calling me for?" he asked. "How can I answer something like that? I'd feel bad if *anyone* did what he did. How do you think the families feel? Do you think they care if he's Jewish?"

The Israeli paper wasn't the only foreign journal interested in the story. Reporters from Australia and Japan were also seen on the corner of Garden and Spruce.

Probably the most-interviewed person in the early days of the story was Michael Brown. He lived a few blocks from the Rifkins. Brown, thirty-five, was honest enough to say from the start that he didn't have much to offer: In the early 1970s he and his sister, Jacque, used to walk to Woodland Junior High School with Joel and Jan Rifkin. Brown had been inside 1492 Garden Street several times. Jeanne Rifkin had given him an occasional English muffin and cup of coffee—made mostly with milk.

That was pretty much it until September 1992. That's when Brown ran into Joel Rifkin again. He, too, was assigned by a temp agency to work at Olympus America.

The two men chatted a few times, mostly commiserating over the low pay—six dollars an hour. Once, Brown gave Rifkin a ride home when Rifkin's truck wasn't working.

Not exactly a best buddy, but Michael Brown was good at giving reporters what they needed: pithy quotes about how surprising all this was, and how Joel Rifkin always seemed to be a quiet, nice man. Besides, when the Rifkin story broke, Michael Brown had another compelling draw for reporters: availability. He hung out in front of 1492 Garden Street all day for almost a week.

It wasn't just news reporters and print journalists—the talk shows, too, were gearing up to cover the Joel Rifkin story. By 10:00 A.M. the day of Rifkin's arraignment, two interns from the *Sally Jessy Raphael* show pulled up in a stretch limousine. When told there had been a flower delivery to the family, courtesy of the *New York Post*, the young women grabbed a local teenager and begged her to help them find the nearest florist. The three disappeared inside the stretch limo and sped off. A short time later they were back. Not long after that came a bigger, more luscious bouquet of flowers.

Watching the interns, a *Newsday* reporter laughed. "I can hear it now," he said, imitating the pitch one of them might use to get them on the show. " 'I myself was a victim, stuck in the house, unable to talk to anyone. If you talk to Sally you'll be okay. She understands. She knows what you're going through.' "

A cameraman turned to the interns and asked the question everyone was thinking. "What's the advantage for these guys to do it?" he said, motioning to the house, where Jeanne and Jan Rifkin remained hidden from the media.

The interns were ready. "Everyone loves Sally," one explained earnestly. "She's compassionate."

Despite the interns' best efforts, Jeanne and Jan Rifkin never appeared on *Sally Jessy*

Raphael. Through Sale they made it clear: they weren't giving interviews.

But Andrea Peyser, a *New York Post* columnist, did manage to land the much-sought-after interview with Jan Rifkin. The serial killer's sister stepped out of the side entrance to the house one evening, not long after the film crews had pulled away. She puffed on a cigarette and walked her cat, Hector, on a long piece of twine.

As Jan and Hector headed down Spruce Lane, Peyser jogged up behind.

"Do you mind if I ask you a few questions?" Peyser asked gently.

Jan eyed her suspiciously. Her eyes were red from crying. She didn't answer.

Peyser tried again. "How are you doing?" she asked.

For a moment there was silence. Peyser waited, walking a few feet behind. The journalist suspected that Jan Rifkin really did want to talk.

Jan Rifkin began to ramble. "He's not evil," she said. "I'm not either. All I can say is I love my brother. I love him."

Peyser nodded. She pulled out her reporter's notepad and began jotting down Jan's words.

Jan Rifkin glanced at her, annoyed. "You just want this for your paper," she said curtly.

Of course, Peyser thought. What does she think?

The columnist tried to soothe the young woman.

"Yes, but don't worry," she said. "You can trust me."

"I don't know," Jan said. "It'll probably be distorted. I can't trust anyone."

She continued to walk Hector. Now and then she exchanged hellos with her neighbors. "We're okay," she called out. "We're doing alright."

Peyser followed behind. "I'm not going to hurt you," the columnist insisted. "I just want to know how he is, how you are."

The journalist bent down and began to pet Hector. Jan Rifkin took another puff of her cigarette and laughed.

"You must be desperate for a story," she said.

Peyser smiled. She continued to pet the cat.

"I'll talk about the cat, okay?" Jan suggested lightly. She gave a gentle tug at Hector's leash and continued to walk down Spruce Lane.

"I love my brother," Jan repeated. "He likes animals. He likes people. He likes everything. I spoke to him on the phone. He's trying to have a life. He's a person. I'm a person."

She told Peyser that she knew something terrible had happened that day when she came home from work. She kept hoping that it was nothing—a traffic ticket—nothing at all.

"I only knew that he was in trouble," she said softly.

Since her brother's arrest, Jan Rifkin couldn't sleep. She and her mother just cried for hours every day. "I'm not really here," she said, her eyes filling with tears. "I keep thinking that I'm really experiencing this, but that I'm really not."

Jan told Peyser she was bitter about the press coverage. After all, she and her mother were at an extremely difficult time in their lives.

"Why don't you put yourself in my shoes?" she said bitterly.

A car door slammed. A reporter from the *Daily News* spotted Jan Rifkin and began to walk toward her. Jan grabbed Hector and sprinted into the house.

Peyser, disappointed at the intrusion, hurried back to her office to write the next day's cover story.

Her chat with Jan Rifkin led the paper the next day.

Jan's words ignited an angry reaction from Jenny Soto's family. Jessy read the paper that morning and threw it on the floor. "Get in your shoes?" she grumbled. "Why doesn't she get in our shoes? Feel how we feel?"

She looked at her baby for a long time and turned to her mother.

"If my son grows up and God forbid I smell something coming from my garage, I'll go check," Jessy said harshly. "And if he has scratches, I'll ask him. That family—they want to be in denial."

Jessy's mother nodded, crying. "If I see his mother, I'll kill her with my own hand," Margarita Gonzalez whispered. "She should know what a lot of mothers are going through."

In general, Jenny Soto's family was unhappy about the media coverage of the case. They ached over a front-page story in the *Daily News* with a large photo of Jenny on the cover. Underneath it read SEX AND DEATH: INSIDE JOEL'S TWISTED WORLD. The story mentioned Jenny's prior arrest for prostitution.

Popcorn came over that day, crying. Jenny's body had been discovered on his birthday; just last month he'd laid a dozen roses at her grave. It was the day she would have turned twenty-four.

All the talk about Jenny being a prostitute stung. He had tried to forget about her earlier arrest. He couldn't—he didn't—believe she'd done it again.

"How could they say those things about her?" Popcorn said. "Don't they know I loved her? She had a boyfriend. I would take care of her if she needed any money. It wasn't like she had to go out on the street."

Jessy nodded. "Mom would have given her money," she said. "Besides, that night she was hanging out with me. She wasn't prostituting. She didn't have to go out there."

Jessy continued to rock her baby. "Even if she did," the young girl added softly, "he didn't have to kill her."

Chapter 16

A week after his arraignment, Joel Rifkin was back in court for a bail hearing. Waiting in the basement courtroom were two women who wanted very much to see him: María Alonso and Margarita Gonzalez. A few of their children sat beside them.

María Alonso had phoned Margarita several days before. When she said who she was—Anna Lopez's mother—Margarita Gonzalez began to weep.

"I know who you are," she said.

For a long time neither woman could speak. They cried on the telephone, sharing their grief. Then María pulled herself together.

"We have to be there, in court," she told Margarita. "We have to see that he doesn't plead insane. We have to make sure everyone understands that he is evil. He's not crazy. He's evil."

Sobbing, Margarita Gonzalez agreed. The two women exchanged information on how to get to Mineola. They decided to meet on the grounds in front of the courthouse, at 262 Old Country Road.

When they did, they embraced warmly. Joel Rifkin was their common enemy: the man who had killed their daughters and shattered their lives.

At the courthouse, journalists surrounded the two mothers.

"I want to see the face of the monster who took my daughter's life," said María. "I wish I had the opportunity to spit on his face."

"Isn't this going to be difficult for you?" she was asked.

María nodded. "This is very painful," she admitted, "but I got through Annie's funeral, I can get through this. We have to show that these girls have families, that they have families who love them and miss them. He is a monster. He is a sadist. If I had the chance, I would kill him myself."

* * *

Shortly before 10:00 A.M., Joel Rifkin was led from the police van into the courthouse. He ducked his head and lifted the middle finger of each hand, giving the throng of photographers an obscene gesture.

The mothers were already in the courtroom. By then, word had spread: Joel Rifkin might not appear for the hearing. Legally, he was required to be in the courthouse, but he was permitted to waive his appearance in court. Rumor was that he had.

María Alonso and Margarita Gonzalez hoped that wasn't true. They'd traveled a long way to see Joel Rifkin. They'd prayed for strength. And they were ready. Each was determined to look into the eyes of her child's killer.

As the two mothers and a crowd of journalists discussed the rumors, court officials got impatient with the noise.

"Want to hold a conversation? Take it outside," they said. "No talking."

María spoke quietly to a reporter from *The New York Times.* "He's not coming, I know it," she said. "I had a feeling this would happen."

The courtroom was called to order. A host

of hearings preceded Joel Rifkin's—mostly burglary and assault cases. Attorneys for the defendants filed various motions and the cases were quickly adjourned.

The only interesting moment came shortly before Joel Rifkin's hearing. Judge Clare Weinberg sharply chastised a young woman who attended her hearing wearing silk shorts.

"When you come back here you dress appropriately," the judge snapped. "This is not a stop on the way to the beach. If I had realized you were wearing shorts, I would not have allowed this adjournment. I would have made you go home and change."

The red-faced young woman nodded. Her attorney gulped. "Judge, I'll further advise her," he said.

Then it was time.

"Number 41. Joel Rifkin," the bailiff said.

The suspense was quickly over. Joel Rifkin did not appear. Robert Sale asked for a postponement, and it was granted. In less than five minutes the hearing was over.

Outside the courtroom, Sale told reporters that his client did not appear in court because prison officials had refused to give him clothes that Sale had provided. Rifkin was wearing an orange jumpsuit supplied by the prison.

"He didn't have appropriate attire," Sale said.

The attorney's explanation didn't sit well with the families of Rifkin's victims. As she filed out of the courtroom, surrounded by press, Margarita Gonzalez became distraught. "He's in the building," she shrieked. "He's hiding!" When asked by reporters what she wanted to say to Rifkin, she began weeping hysterically: "Kill him. That's all I want. That you kill him!"

Outside, she and María Alonso waited more than five hours on the grass by the prison van. They were determined to see Joel Rifkin, even if it was for the few seconds it took him to walk from the courthouse to the van.

As they waited the two mothers linked arms and talked quietly in Spanish. They took off their shoes. At one point, María fixed Margie's hair in a bun. María's daughters, Claudia and Monica, picked up lunch at a nearby deli.

Their long wait proved pointless. After promising the mothers that they would bring Joel Rifkin out the usual way, court officers slipped him out through another exit. Reporters were annoyed—they'd been waiting for the dramatic confrontation. When asked why the change, court officers said they thought it would be too emotional for the mothers; they thought it was better this way.

María Alonso and Margarita Gonzalez did not agree. But they said they would be back. Eventually they would confront their daughters' killer. They were determined.

A week later, Joel Rifkin was indicted for the murder of Tiffany Bresciani. A grand jury listened to evidence provided by detectives and the prosecutor. It didn't take long for the jurors to bring back a true bill.

The next day, Nassau County District Attorney Denis Dillon held a press conference at the Mineola courthouse. In addition to Dillon, Captain Walter Heesch, the head of the Rifkin investigation, and Fred Klein, the assistant DA prosecuting the case, were on hand.

"We called you here to announce the filing of a three-count indictment charging Joel Rikfin with two counts of murder in the second degree and one count of reckless endangerment in the first degree," Dillon said.

The DA went on to explain the specifics: The first murder count was for intentionally causing the death of Tiffany Bresciani; the second, for a depraved indifference to human life. The third count, reckless endangerment, alleged that Joel Rifkin created a risk to state troopers by leading them on a high-speed chase through the streets of Nassau County.

When he was finished, reporters began to call out questions. Dillon held up his hand.

"I'm not going to get into any other crimes that may have been committed other than the one that is subject to this indictment, and I'm not going to get into evidence. But ask your questions."

Reporters laughed. That didn't leave them much room.

Someone asked why there was just one indictment. What about all the other women Rifkin had confessed to killing?

"Nassau has jurisdiction over this case because the body was found here," Dillon explained. "When state police have completed their investigation and information is taken to DAs in different jurisdictions, they can bring their charges whenever they are ready."

Roger Stern from WNBC spoke next.

"Thinking back to other serial killers—they're almost never prosecuted on all the murders they allegedly committed. From a prosecutor's standpoint, is there a law of diminishing returns? You only go for your best cases?"

Dillon was vague. "It's tough to compare one serial killer with another and the crimes they committed," he said. "In some situations you have strong evidence that can be presented, and you have a very good chance of getting a conviction. Some of the other cases might be less. In terms of this series of possible prosecutions there will be discussions, I'm sure, between the state police and the various prosecutors and, if necessary, our office."

"The defense attorney has suggested he may try an insanity plea," a radio reporter called out.

"That's the job of a defense attorney—to do everything he can to ensure his client gets justice, whatever he feels is justice in a particular circumstance," Dillon answered smoothly. "It requires him to raise whatever defense he feels necessary."

"What do you have to prove [in order] to prove you are insane?" Roger Stern asked.

"The defense requires that he did not understand the nature and consequences of his act, or that the conduct was wrong."

Stern pushed harder. "The material found at his house documenting all of his alleged victims, a book on another serial killer—would that imply that this was a man grounded in reality who knew what he was doing?"

But Dillon couldn't be budged. "I'm not going to get into a discussion on what was found at the house and certainly not any conclusion that can be drawn from it."

Another reporter tried a similar approach. "What about the talk of a possible copycat—that he may have been motivated or influenced by those Green River killings in Seattle?"

Dillon sighed. He wasn't going to give in.

"I don't think it's helpful, at least at this time, to speculate about those things," he said. "We're here to announce this particular indictment."

223

"What motivated him?" the same reporter asked.

Dillon shook his head. "We're here to announce this particular indictment," he repeated.

"Have you brought in psychiatric experts to give you advice on—"

Dillon cut off the reporter. "We're not going to talk about any step so far on the investigation," he said. "We're not going to speculate. We're just here to talk about the indictment."

"Can you characterize the case that you have against him, that you're indicting him on?"

"No, it's not proper for me to characterize."

"Would you characterize it as strong?"

"I'm not going to characterize it, except to say that the grand jury found the evidence was sufficient to return an indictment."

Reporters moved on to Walter Heesch. Perhaps, they thought, the police spokesman would be a bit more helpful.

He wasn't. The captain carefully spoke without saying much of anything.

"What do these things indicate to you about this man's motivations—a book on another serial killer, books on tying ropes, the collecting of these things?" he was asked.

"At this stage of the investigation, we can only speculate," Heesch responded. "It wouldn't do us any good to give a statement on this now."

"We understand he had a book on ropes and knots. Did he tie up his victims?"

"I can't comment on that."

"Why do you believe that it's going to be close to the seventeen, eighteen figure? Why do you believe that it's not going to be thirty-four or fifty, but that he seems to have kept track?"

"Well, after the initial findings there was no other evidence to indicate more than seventeen or eighteen. We're going based on the facts we have now."

"Captain, there was a matter of him losing count, and not lying—"

"I don't think he was lying," Captain Heesch said. "I simply think he may have lost count. I don't know if it was seventeen or eighteen. But we have what we have."

The men thanked the press. The news conference was over.

* * *

Two days later, Joel Rifkin was arraigned on the two counts of second-degree murder and the reckless endangerment charge. This time, María Alonso and Margarita Gonzalez knew, he would appear in court. They would too.

Reporters gathered outside Judge Ira Wexner's chambers on the first floor of the courthouse. It was stifling in the crowded hallway.

"Why can't we sit inside, in the air-conditioning?" a reporter asked.

"Why?" quipped Court Officer Franzone. "Why does a whale have a small hole on top of his head? Because that's just the way it is."

Franzone clapped his hands to get the crowd's attention.

"Seats will be given on a first-come, first-served basis," he announced. "Please form a line."

As reporters jockeyed for position, someone tried again.

"Can you ask the judge if we can wait inside?"

"That I can do," the court officer said. He disappeared into Wexner's chambers.

A few minutes later Franzone returned. He

opened the courtroom door and stepped back.

"You can wait inside," he said. "But you have to leave when the defendant is brought in. Don't bother to fight for prime seats. It's not going to matter."

María Alonso paid no attention. "Where will he be?" she asked aloud, peering at the bench. "I want to make sure I see him."

For the next half hour, María sat quietly, staring straight ahead. A few rows away, Margarita Gonzalez sat with her daughter, Margie, and read the Bible. All around them reporters chatted, sharing gossip.

"Did you hear Mary Jo Buttafuoco's comment on Joel?" one said to a row of journalists. "She said, 'All these detectives were chasing my husband for statutory rape when this guy's killing girls and dumping them.' "

The small group nodded. All the Long Island reporters were following the Amy-Joey epic closely.

Bored, one reporter began a wish list.

"I hope Rifkin goes crazy right here," she said. "I hope he turns around and scratches his own eyeballs. And I hope he turns to the judge and says, 'You're next.' "

The others laughed.

"Any good Rifkin jokes?" a print reporter asked.

"I heard one," a colleague answered. "What's Joel Rifkin's line when he tries to pick up girls?"

Silence.

"I dig you."

Groans were heard.

"How about this?" the reporter tried again. "Hear Joel Rifkin got an American Express card? It's for dismembers only."

A little after 10:00 A.M. the judge was ready. The courtroom was cleared as Joel Rifkin was brought in, his hands cuffed in front. The prison orange was gone; he wore a gray striped shirt and gray slacks. He sat silently with his attorney, looking down. As scores of journalists and onlookers attempted to reenter the room, court officers tried to keep order.

"Form a line," Franzone called out. "We need a line."

It was useless. The crush of media jammed through the door. By the time María Alonso and Margarita Gonzalez managed to push their way inside, all the seats close to the front were taken.

They took seats in the third-to-last row. Margarita immediately opened the Bible and began to read. Her daughter, Margie, sighed when asked by reporters how her mother was handling the stress.

"I don't know why she wants to be here," she said. "I keep telling her—"

"All rise," the bailiff announced.

There were a few procedural motions, and a date was set for the next hearing: August 16. And then, the plea.

"To the charges, murder in the second degree; reckless endangerment. How do you plead?"

Joel Rifkin's voice echoed in the silent courtroom. "I am not guilty," he said.

For only a moment there was no sound. Then, in the third-to-last row, the weeping began.

"Killer, killer," Margarita Gonzalez said, rocking in her seat, clenching the Bible to her chest. "You killed my daughter. Kill him, kill him."

"Quiet," court officers said. "Clear the courtroom."

Margarita's sobs grew louder. Led by a

court officer, she slowly made her way down
the aisle toward the door near the defendant's table. María Alonso followed, crying
softly.

The man who had killed their daughters
remained seated, next to his attorney. As
they filed past him, the mothers stopped.
They could see only his profile, and even that
was partly obstructed by Sale and court officers. But it was him: Joel Rifkin. They had
at last glimpsed the face of the monster.

Outside the courtroom, the mothers continued to weep. María managed to slip away,
but Margarita was not as fortunate. She and
Margie tried to leave, but couldn't. Dozens of
reporters encircled them, hungry for quotes.

"Mrs. Gonzalez, it must have been very
difficult for you," they said, jamming microphones in front of her.

"Are you satisfied? At least you got the
chance—"

"How do you feel?"

"What would you like to say to Joel Rifkin?"

Margarita Gonzalez pushed through the
crush, nearly hysterical. At that point some

reporters stepped back. "This is so unnecessary," said one. "It's cruel."

Her arm around her mother, Margie Gonzalez lost her patience and screamed at reporters. "Take it easy," she yelled. "Don't act like animals!"

Turning to her mother, she ducked her head and said softly, "Okay, Mom? You want to talk or not?"

Margarita Gonzalez shook her head. "Let's go home," she whispered.

A court officer came to their rescue.

"Where are you going?" he asked.

"To the train," Margie said.

His hand resting on Margarita Gonzalez's shoulder, the officer led mother and daughter down the steps of the courthouse, across the grass, and a few blocks away, to the Long Island Rail Road station. A few reporters tagged along, but by then the crowd had broken.

On the train ride home, Margarita Gonzalez leaned her head against the window. She closed her eyes. She saw Jenny's face. Then she saw the face of her daughter's killer.

Anguish consumed Margarita Gonzalez.

Chapter 17

IN the days following Joel Rifkin's arrest, police had interviewed numerous prostitutes on the streets of Manhattan. The cops learned that Joel Rifkin's pickup truck was a familiar sight on Twelfth Street and Second Avenue and at the corner of Allen Street and Rivington. The descriptions the young women gave were often similar: as the Mazda slowly cruised the streets, Joel Rifkin had carefully inspected each girl. He always took a long time to choose.

Was he deciding whom he wanted to die?

Perhaps. Yet not every one of his encounters with a prostitute led to murder. In fact, some women on the streets remembered Joel Rifkin as an ordinary, even gentle customer.

Experts aren't surprised. They say that serial killers are often satiated after a murder; indeed, Joel Rifkin may have gone months without the desire to kill. Examining trophies—the credit cards, panties, and jewelry of previous victims—may have been enough to satisfy him.

But as the weeks passed, his lethal craving likely grew. And so Joel Rifkin would strike again. And again. His deadly tally climbed.

One woman survived two encounters with Joel Rifkin. She calls herself Charlotte Webb. She is twenty-seven years old, an emaciated heroin addict who works the streets of lower Manhattan. Despite the unremitting anguish of her life on the street, Charlotte Webb remains in many ways the young woman she was before heroin: warm and garrulous. She considers herself very lucky that she is not one of Joel Rifkin's eighteen victims.

Charlotte began turning tricks when she was twenty. She was an exotic dancer, and for a while she worked in a New Jersey brothel. But in recent years she has been working the street, mostly around Allen Street and Rivington. In some ways, she is more fortunate than many prostitutes she knows: Charlotte has an apartment. It is a cramped, cluttered studio, but it is her own.

Joel Rifkin first approached Charlotte Webb in March or April of 1993. By then, his killing spree was nearing its end. He'd strangled at least seventeen women.

It was late morning. Charlotte was strolling Twelfth Street and Second Avenue. She was waiting impatiently for a client. She needed a fix.

The pickup slowed down. Joel Rifkin leaned out the window.

"Have you been working the street a long time?" he called.

Charlotte thought fast. The guy probably wanted a girl with experience—someone who was good at what she did, Charlotte thought. "Oh, yes," she answered brightly. "I've been working quite a while."

Joel Rifkin looked disappointed. "Well, no. I'm not looking for that," he said. "I'm looking for someone who hasn't been working a long time."

He began to inspect the other women on the street. "What about that girl, the one over there?" he said, pointing. "Do you know about her? Has she been working long?"

Charlotte tried to help. She perused the

street, telling the man in the pickup about a few of the other girls. He drove off, and Charlotte leaned against a building. Can't please everybody, she thought.

Over the next few weeks, Charlotte noticed the Mazda pickup a few more times. She thought it odd how carefully the driver looked before he chose a date. Most men did inspect the girls, of course, but there was something different here. She shrugged it off. He would probably never stop for her again anyway.

A month later, however, he did. Charlotte was working a different area—Allen Street. That, and Twelfth and Second, were the only twenty-four-hour strolls in the city.

It was about noon. The Mazda slowed down.

"You been working the streets long?" Joel Rifkin asked.

Charlotte smiled. He didn't remember her from the last time. And now she was prepared.

She shook her head emphatically. "Oh, I just did it a few times last summer," she said. "I haven't been doing this long. Pretty new at it, actually."

"Alright, get in," Rifkin said.

Charlotte climbed inside. The cab of the truck was a mess. She looked at Rifkin. He was too. Charlotte moved her feet gingerly, pushing aside the trash. Hopefully, she thought, this will be quick.

"What do you charge?" Rifkin asked.

Charlotte didn't hesitate. "What do you think is reasonable?" she said smoothly.

It was her standard line. She had to be cautious. First of all, she didn't want to name a price that was too high and scare the customer away. She didn't want to make an offer that was too low, either. Besides, you never could be too sure. The client could be an undercover cop.

Charlotte had had a few experiences in the past in which potential clients refused to make the first offer. The men would go back and forth with her for a while, but Charlotte never gave in. In the end, she would simply refuse the job.

"If you're not willing to cooperate with me, and give me something I can say yes or no to, I might think you're a cop," she'd say.

Once the man really was a cop. He had laughed.

"You deserve not to get busted because you're smart," he said.

Things went more smoothly with Joel Rifkin. He immediately offered his price.

"How about forty bucks?" he said.

Charlotte agreed. It wasn't a great rate, but it would do.

"Okay, forty," she said. "Maybe you'll give me a tip if you like me in the end."

Rifkin nodded. He put the truck in gear.

"I have an apartment," Charlotte said. "It would be a lot safer."

"Is anyone there?" Rifkin asked.

"No, I live alone."

Charlotte gave him directions. Rifkin drove about a mile uptown and parked, just a few doors from a local police precinct.

On the way, they talked. Rifkin said his name was Jimmy. He was married, but going through a divorce. He had kids in college. It was a struggle to pay for their education.

Charlotte thought he seemed nice. "You seem lonely, like me," she told him. "Well, you've got a friend. You can trust me."

Joel Rifkin smiled at Charlotte Webb. "You're nice," he said. "You're different than other girls."

"Well, I like to be friends with people," she said, returning the smile.

They went to her apartment. Charlotte Webb undressed and climbed into bed. She handed him a condom.

It was over quickly.

Normal, gentle, simple sex, Charlotte thought. An easy forty dollars.

As he dressed, Joel Rifkin told Charlotte he'd like to see her again. The young woman wrote down her name and address on a scrap of paper. She didn't have a phone, she explained. It kept getting turned off.

"Come see me anytime," she said, as he left. "You've got a friend."

A few weeks later, less than a month before he killed Tiffany Bresciani, Joel Rifkin returned to Allen Street. When he spotted Charlotte, she waved. He unlocked the door of the pickup. She climbed in the car.

"I came back for you," Joel Rifkin said.

Charlotte smiled. "Do you mind if I make a stop?" she asked.

Rifkin said he didn't mind. He drove her to the corner of Clinton and Houston Streets and gave her the forty-dollar fee in advance. Charlotte disappeared for a few minutes. When she returned, she'd bought a half ounce of cocaine and two single portions of heroin.

"A lot of girls might have ripped you off," she told Rifkin as she climbed back in the pickup. "I'm not like that."

They went to her apartment. Charlotte slipped into the bathroom and did a speedball. Then they had sex. Once again it was uneventful. If Joel Rifkin had murderous intents, he didn't show them.

They talked again, for almost half an hour. Charlotte told Rifkin she liked photography.

"See how big my hands are?" she said, holding them up. "I need an Olympus camera. It's the most comfortable for my hands. A lot of people go for the camera by its brand name, but I go by the way it fits in my hands."

"I work for Olympus," Rifkin told her. "I do distribution. I could probably get you a discount on a camera."

"That'd be great," Charlotte said.

She didn't believe him. She didn't think he really worked for Olympus, and if he did, she certainly didn't expect any camera discounts. She didn't mind, though. In her business, Charlotte didn't expect to hear much of anything that was true.

The next time Charlotte Webb saw Joel Rifkin his picture was plastered on the front page of all the New York City dailies. Two days after Rifkin's arrest, Charlotte was home, sleeping, when the buzzer rang.

She didn't answer it. She never did. It could be a cop.

It wasn't. It was Russell Ben-Ali, a *Newsday* reporter, and his photographer. They'd been given a tip from a state police investigator. The name Charlotte Webb, with a midtown Manhattan address, had been found in Joel Rifkin's bedroom.

When he got the lead, Ben-Ali had immediately headed uptown from his office. Charlotte Webb was probably another victim, he figured. But the cops had said they thought she lived with a boyfriend, a man named Jeffrey. Perhaps, the reporter thought, the boyfriend would consent to an interview.

When he arrived at the building, Ben-Ali buzzed the bell with the name Jeffrey next to it. Silence. He tried again.

"Maybe it's not working," he said to the photographer.

The two men decided to wait. Ben-Ali had been chasing leads on the Rifkin case for several days. This one seemed as if it had potential.

After about half an hour, a neighbor opened the door. Ben-Ali slipped in and knocked at the apartment number he'd been given by police.

Again, silence. He knocked a bit harder.

Charlotte was groggy from sleep. She roused herself and pulled on some clothes. "Who is it?" she called out.

Ben-Ali was taken aback. He hadn't expected to hear a woman's voice; he assumed Charlotte was a victim.

"I'm looking for Jeffrey, or else someone who might know Charlotte," he said.

"Well, I'm Charlotte," the voice sang out. "Who are you?"

Ben-Ali was even more surprised. There must be some mistake, he thought. Charlotte was supposed to be dead.

"I'm a reporter from *Newsday*," he said. "My name's Russell Ben-Ali."

Charlotte still wasn't ready to open the door. "Are you with that guy from the *Village Voice*?" she asked. "You know, he's doing a book on me."

"No, I'm not affiliated with him," Ben-Ali explained. "I'm from *Newsday*. We're doing a story on Joel Rifkin."

At last the door opened.

"Really," Charlotte said, her eyes widening. "I've been waiting to talk to someone about that. I didn't know if the police would believe me. When I saw the picture of the pickup truck, I thought it might be him."

Ben-Ali and his photographer entered the apartment. For the next ten minutes Charlotte chatted easily about Joel Rifkin. Wasn't that amazing, she said. She wondered if she knew any of the women he'd killed. Now that she thought about it, Charlotte told the reporter, a few of her friends might be missing. This girl named Angie. Or was it Chelsea?

Suddenly, Charlotte Webb stopped. Until now she hadn't realized the danger she had been in.

"How did you get my name?" she asked breathlessly.

"We got a tip from a detective," Ben-Ali said. "Your name and address were found in Joel Rifkin's house."

Suddenly it came together. Charlotte got up and began walking in circles around her tiny apartment.

"My God," she practically screamed. "It could have been me. It could have been me. I can't believe I'm alive. I can't believe it."

For the next few hours Russell Ben-Ali tried to get Charlotte to remember her past encounters with Joel Rifkin. It was no easy task. Charlotte regularly trailed off onto other topics. Ben-Ali did his best to help her focus on Joel Rifkin.

By the time he left, the reporter had only half an hour before the evening's deadline. Back in the office, Ben-Ali wrote his story speedily. The next day Charlotte Webb made the cover of *Newsday*. She was pictured leaning reflectively on the windowsill of her apartment. The quote above her said it plainly: MY GOD, IT COULD HAVE BEEN ME.

Charlotte Webb was delighted. She called her parents to make sure they'd bought the paper. She shot heroin. It was almost 4:00 P.M. before she returned home. When she did, two detectives were waiting. They had been camped out in front of her building for several hours.

The cops didn't look twice as Charlotte brushed past them and unlocked the front door. "Idiots," Charlotte mumbled to herself when the cops still didn't recognize her.

She turned and smiled broadly. "Hi, I'm Charlotte," she said. "Are you looking for me?"

"Oh, yes," one said, clearly uncomfortable.

The two men showed their identification. O'Neill and Harris. New York State Police.

"We're not here to bust you," one said.

"I would expect not," Charlotte quipped. "Come on in."

They followed her inside. The detectives stood awkwardly in the small room.

"Why don't you sit?" Charlotte said.

"No thanks," one said. "We're okay."

Charlotte tried again. "I have a real nice rocking chair here," she said, pushing the chair with her foot. "You sure?"

They were.

Guess they don't want to seem too off-duty, Charlotte thought.

One of the men pulled out a photograph.

"Is this you?" he asked.

Charlotte looked at the image carefully.

"It isn't me," she said finally. "It looks like my friend Angie. She's been missing for a while. I keep asking people, 'Where's Angie?'"

The cops showed her another picture. It was a young girl sitting on a fire hydrant.

"Is this the same girl?" he asked.

"I don't know," she said. "But that's definitely not Angie,"

The detectives exchanged glances. Charlotte caught on quickly. "You're just testing me," she said, laughing. "You want to make sure I'm telling the truth."

For the next fifteen minutes, the detectives asked her about Joel Rifkin. Charlotte told them what she recalled. Then they gave her their business cards.

"You'll call us if you think of anything else?" one asked. "And please give us a number when you get your phone hooked up."

Charlotte promised she would. She closed the door and breathed a sigh of relief. The less contact with cops, the better, she thought.

Seconds later the detectives knocked again. Charlotte got nervous. Great, now they're going to arrest me, she thought.

"What do you want?" she called out through the door.

"One more question," one detective said. "Do you recall a tattoo on Joel's chest?"

Charlotte made a face behind the door. "No, I don't recall any tattoo."

No answer. A few seconds later she heard the outside door open and close. Testing me again, she thought to herself.

Over the next few weeks Charlotte heard a lot of girls on the street claimed they had "dated" Joel Rifkin. She never challenged them. She just laughed to herself.

"They haven't, but I really have," she told a reporter. "Know what's funny? I think they're rather jealous of me."

Chapter 18

RADIO talk show hosts couldn't get enough of the Joel Rifkin story. Shock jock host Howard Stern of radio station WXRK talked about little else for the week following Rifkin's arrest.

He interviewed Rifkin's neighbors, childhood friends, and former employers. He poked fun at Jeanne Rifkin, describing the elderly widow as walking around in a daze and continuing to putter around in her garden.

One caller who lived down the block from the Rifkins said that Joel Rifkin seemed odd and always looked and smelled dirty. The caller said that he frequently saw Rifkin working on his trucks late at night, and that many in the neighborhood thought it strange.

"It was just so bizarre," the caller said. "One day, the car would be working for a couple of days, then he puts it up on those stilt type of things and takes out parts and transfers it to the other car and drives that one around. Half the week one car would be working, the other half the other car. . . . Two frames, one car."

"That's a dead giveaway," Stern said firmly. "There's no normal guy doing that."

The caller continued. He said that the day before Rifkin's arrest, he saw him working on his Mazda.

"My wife said, 'What do you think of him,' " the caller recounted. "I said, 'Oh, keep away from him. I don't want you to talk to him. I don't want you to look at him. He's nuts. You never know about this guy.' "

"Well, I'll tell you something," Stern shot back. "I saw that garden on TV. That's the work of a mental patient. He has all kinds of trails and everything . . . It looks like a nightmare garden . . . like a Chinese warlord garden."

* * *

Over the next few days the phone lines were
jammed with callers trying to get into the
spotlight. Employees from Record World
phoned in. So did former classmates at East
Meadow High School.

Over at Spirit Insurance in East Meadow,
the staff was excited. They, too, wanted to go
on the air and talk to Stern. After all, they
had as much right as anyone: Joel Rifkin
was a customer. He insured his Mazda with
Spirit.

The morning after Rifkin's arrest, shortly
after 7:00 A.M., Spirit customer service rep-
resentative Dawn Kessler had opened the office and gone directly to the files.

She'd heard Rifkin's name on the news.

That name is so familiar, she thought. I
bet he has insurance with us.

Alone in the office, Kessler hunted
through the files. She found his at once.

I knew it, she thought.

Thumbing through his papers, she tried to
remember her dealings with Joel Rifkin.
He'd first signed up at Spirit on December 3,
1992, wanting in insure a 1976 Mercury
sedan. Spirit had quoted Rifkin a price—
$750 annually—but a few weeks later it was

raised to $893. Rifkin hadn't told them about an accident he'd had a few years earlier.

Three weeks later Rifkin showed up again. He wanted to switch his policy, putting the same license plates on his gray Mazda pickup.

Dawn had helped him. She remembered how he'd stared at her and the other girls in the office. Once Dawn's future brother-in-law, Mike Lomelo, who also worked at Spirit, had caught her eye and motioned to Rifkin. "That guy's a psycho," Mike had whispered. Dawn had nodded, rolling her eyes.

On April 5 Rifkin had had an accident with a Bellmore man. He told Dawn that his pickup truck had fallen out of gear and smashed into a car. The damage to the pickup was minimal, but the other car's right rear door and quarter panel were bent. Rifkin got an estimate from a body shop: $1,338.

For more than a week, Dawn had spoken to Rifkin almost daily, calling him at his job at Olympus. She'd helped him fill out the proper forms. When he came in to the office, Dawn had tried not to notice how he looked at her.

She glanced at the file again. Rifkin's insurance had been canceled on May 20, more than a month before. He'd failed to make his last two payments.

Alone at Spirit, Dawn Kessler suddenly felt strange. She thought about the way Joel Rifkin had eyed her. Could I have been one of those girls? she wondered. Dawn put the file away. In a short time, a few of the other employees arrived. She didn't mention Joel Rifkin.

A few hours later, Dawn was at her desk, sending bills, when the front door burst open. It was Spirit owner John Rose. Everyone in the office looked up.

"Quick, give me the murderer's file!" he yelled. He had been listening to Howard Stern on the drive into work. Stern had been complaining about the lack of callers who actually knew Joel Rifkin.

Dawn began to laugh. "I know, I know," she said, holding up the file. "Can you believe this?"

John grabbed it. He searched through the pages until he found what he was looking for: a copy of Rifkin's driver's license. He ran to the copy machine and made an enlarged copy. He quickly scribbled a note: "To Howard Stern from Spirit Agency Insurance in

East Meadow. Serial killer was insured here. We have all the psychos."

John Rose faxed the note to *The Howard Stern Show*. He yelled at one of his employees, Garrett Duffy, to get the show on the line.

"Did you know about this, Dawn?" John asked.

"Yeah, I pulled the file," she said. "I remember helping him. Maybe just a month ago."

"It's Spirit Insurance," Duffy said, into the phone. "The murderer had insurance here." Within minutes, Howard Stern's producer, Gary Dell'abate, was on the line.

"We're putting you on the air," he said. "Put on someone who had dealings with the killer."

John Rose immediately turned to Dawn. "You do it," he practically commanded. "You're the last one who had contact with him."

Dawn agreed. She called her fiancé, Ray Lomelo, and her brother. "I'm going to be on the radio," she said, rushed. "Quick, turn it on."

She hung up. Suddenly she began to get nervous. She knew the way Stern taunted his guests. "I don't know," Dawn began saying, her confidence wilting. "What am I going to say? What's Howard going to do to me? What if he starts being obnoxious to me?"

Her coworkers tried to reassure her. "Don't worry, you'll be great," they said.

Dell'abate called back.

"Five minutes," he said.

"Five minutes," John Rose sang out.

The owner of Spirit Insurance Agency began to dance around the room. "We're going to be on *The Howard Stern Show*, we're going on *Howard*," he chanted.

He turned to face his employees. Everyone was laughing.

"You know, every day I think, Who are these morons who call Howard Stern?" John said. "And here we are—we're one of those morons!"

The radio interview lasted just a few minutes. Dawn Kessler told Stern what she remembered—Joel Rifkin had acted strangely, and always leered at her and the other girls in the office.

HOWARD: Did he try to bite you?

DAWN: No, but was staring at all the girls in the office.

253

HOWARD: I see. I see.

DAWN: We have a lot of pretty girls who work here.

HOWARD: Are you pretty?

DAWN: Oh yeah.

HOWARD: Oh really?

DAWN: Oh yeah.

Dawn went on to describe the accident Joel Rifkin had had in April. She said he told her that his pickup had somehow fallen out of gear and hit another car.

DAWN: He kept saying how crazy the other guy was.

HOWARD: And was he looking at you?

DAWN: Oh, yeah.

HOWARD: He was taking you in.

DAWN: He was just eyeballing everybody.

HOWARD: To the audience at home, you're a very attractive woman?

DAWN: Oh yeah.

HOWARD: What do you look like, facially? Farrah Fawcett Majors?

DAWN: I would say more like Goldie Hawn.

HOWARD: Oh really. You got a body like her?

DAWN: Yeah.

HOWARD: Was this Rifkin character trying to come on to you?

DAWN: He was . . . I would say he stared at me the whole time.

HOWARD: You were really turned off to him?

DAWN: Completely.

HOWARD: He made your skin crawl. . . . Were you wearing a miniskirt the day he came in?

DAWN: I think I was wearing a minidress the day he came in.

HOWARD: He was staring at your legs?

DAWN: Head to toe.

HOWARD: Soaking you in . . . He didn't say anything weird to you, like, "I have to bury you"?

DAWN: No, he just said he wanted to insure the car because he wanted to drive his friends around.

HOWARD: Well, he sure did. One more thing. Did he try to stuff you in a garbage bag?

DAWN: No. He didn't have a chance.

When it was over, everyone at Spirit hugged Dawn at once.

"You were great," they kept shouting. "Great!"

"I didn't sound good," Dawn said immediately. "My voice sounded so deep—boyish like."

"You sounded great," they kept telling her. "You're a star."

The phones didn't stop ringing all day. Customers and friends called to say they'd heard the show. The Federal Express delivery man was impressed. "Who's Dawn? Who's Dawn?" he kept asking.

Even the mailman stopped by. It was his day off. He'd been washing his car in the driveway, listening to the radio. He'd been laughing all morning.

"That was the funniest thing I ever heard," he told John Rose.

The next morning, Dawn Kessler opened Spirit as usual. But this time the young woman felt a bit uncomfortable. She was glad Joel Rifkin wasn't out on bail.

I wonder if he heard me on the radio, she thought. Here I am, in his office by myself.

Dawn brushed off the disturbing images. He's not getting out of jail, she thought. Not ever.

Chapter 19

AS of this writing, Joel Rifkin is being held in protective custody in Building B of the Nassau County Correctional Facility, not far from the cell where Amy Fisher was imprisoned. Rifkin's six-by-nine foot cell has a bunk and a commode. It faces a corridor, so he is watched by corrections officers at all times.

In jail, Rifkin reads newspapers and watches accounts of himself from a television in the lobby. He eats a muffin, cereal, and fruit for breakfast. Sometimes he has hot dogs and baked beans for lunch, spaghetti, veal patty and green beans for dinner. Officials say he is a quiet inmate.

He meets frequently with Robert Sale. They discuss what exactly Rifkin told investigators and how the attorney plans to defend him. Sale explains pending motions and what they mean for Rifkin's defense.

Under state criminal procedure law, a murder case can be prosecuted in the county where a killing occurred or where the body was found. In Rifkin's case, the bodies of the fourteen victims that have been linked to him are spread over nine New York State counties: New York County (Manhattan), Kings (Brooklyn), Queens, Bronx, Nassau, Suffolk, Westchester, Orange, and Putnam. Police are still searching in the Nyack and Harriman areas of Rockland County, in New York City, and in New Jersey for four missing bodies.

In mid-July Sale proposed that the nine counties consolidate their cases and hold a single trial in one county on all charges. The advantage of a single trial is that Sale would have to convince only one jury that his client did not commit these murders, or, as is the more likely scenario, that his client was not responsible for his actions.

Technically, state law precludes such a joint trial; however, district attorneys have the discretionary authority to approve it. In this case, though, most of the prosecutors rejected the suggestion outright. It was a blow to Sale's defense, although not an unexpected one.

So now, a squadron of prosecutors is attempting to sort out where Joel Rifkin will be tried and in what order to bring the cases. The prosecutors must be careful: Their first case against Rifkin should be the strongest, since an acquittal in the first trial could weaken all the other trials. They must also take pains to avoid ego rivalries over the case. No doubt few prosecutors would willingly yield authority in such a high-profile case. To win the murder conviction that sends Joel Rifkin to prison would surely bolster any prosecutor's career.

It is almost unquestionable that the first trial—the one with the strongest evidence—will be for the killing of Tiffany Bresciani. Prosecutors can directly implicate Rifkin through the finding of Tiffany's body in the truck. A trial is expected to be held in early 1994 in Nassau County, where the body was discovered.

Sale is currently mapping out his defense strategy. He will surely try to suppress the statements Joel Rifkin gave to investigators.

The attorney will argue that without a videotaped confession, or a written account of the crimes, his client should not be held to verbal admissions.

An insanity defense is almost guaranteed. But with it goes a rigorous fight. To be acquitted under such a plea, the defense has to prove that at the time of each murder, the suspect was suffering from a mental disease or defect, and failed to know or appreciate that what he was doing was morally wrong.

Sale will attempt to prove it. He's done it before. In the mid-1970s he won an acquittal for Mate Ivanov of Mineola. Ivanov, who spoke seven languages and had an IQ of 165, admitted chopping up his wife, three children, and the family dog with a bayonet. He fled to Florida and attempted to swim to Cuba. At the trial, a host of psychiatrists testified that Ivanov was sane.

But Robert Sale convinced a jury otherwise. Mate Ivanov was found not guilty by reason of insanity, and now lives freely in France. Sale calls his former client a productive person. He says Ivanov keeps in touch with him.

Prosecutors want to ensure that Joel Rifkin never goes free. They will likely fight an insanity defense by calling psychiatrists to testify that Joel Rifkin knew that what he was doing was wrong. They will certainly point out that Rifkin methodically planned the murders and the disposal of the bodies, and that he tried to conceal his link to the victims. Additionally, Rifkin has not shown any sign of mental disturbance while in custody. And he does not have a lengthy record of psychiatric problems.

As the legal system presses its case against Joel Rifkin, state police officials have unfinished work. As of this writing they continue to hunt for the four bodies they have not yet found but believe are Rifkin victims. And they still don't know the identities of three of the bodies they already have.

Colonel Wayne Bennett, head of the New York State Police Bureau of Criminal Investigation, is not optimistic. "Without the further cooperation of Mr. Rifkin, we may never make a positive identification," he has said. "We have no names, only approximate dates, approximate circumstances and locations. It's not precise enough."

About a week after the arrest, state police went back to 1492 Garden Street. Several days before, they had identified the body of the eighteenth Rifkin victim—Mary Catherine Williams—the one Rifkin never mentioned. With that new information, cops requested and were granted a second search warrant. They combed the house again.

This time, investigators gathered several used condoms and a hypodermic needle and syringe, believed to have been from one of the victims. They also took more mundane household items—sheets, towels, pillowcases, typewriter ribbons, plastic wrap, books, magazines, a shower curtain, even a barbecue grill cover.

From the garage, they collected axes, machetes, pruning shears, a chain saw, a sickle, a coping saw, a knife, and duct tape. They removed a stain sample from the garage floor, which they believe to be blood.

They are looking for traces of blood or hair on the items that may be linked to victims. Once the evidence has been examined, state police officials will decide whether to submit it for DNA analysis.

It continues to be a protracted investigation. Interestingly, officials of the New York State Police have not asked for help from the FBI's Behavioral Science Unit in Quantico,

Virginia. They have chosen, instead, to handle the case themselves.

The reason may date back to the handling of the Arthur Shawcross case. Sources say that in the case of the Rochester serial killer, state police did a thorough investigation, only to see the FBI's BSU take credit. Traditionally, the FBI has been criticized for stepping over smaller police units.

"The FBI did not contribute what they claimed," a law enforcement source said. "The whole philosophy of that unit is to help police and not steal the thunder. They blew it with Shawcross. They made public claims that they solved the case. And they didn't. The state police did."

Whoever uncovers the truth, Joel Rifkin will likely go down in the annals of history as one of the most prolific serial killers. He joins a grim team.

Of all sentenced serial killers, John Wayne Gacy still holds the record for the most convictions. On March 12, 1980, a Chicago jury found him guilty of murdering thirty-three young men.

Twenty-nine of Gacy's victims were buried in the crawl space beneath his Norwood

Park, Illinois, home. Nine bodies were never identified.

John Wayne Gacy was a well-known and active member of his community. He was a construction contractor, a part-time clown, and a Democratic precinct captain. But the short, stocky man had a nefarious side. His killing spree began in 1973, when he lured a sixteen-year-old boy to his ranch-style home and strangled him.

For the next five years, Gacy coaxed young men, often his own employees, to his home and forced them to have sex. He often tricked them into letting him put a pair of handcuffs on their wrists. He tortured them until he grew tired.

Then he murdered them. He told police he strangled each one by wrapping rope around the boy's neck and twisting it with a stick. After he killed the young men, he would often sleep with the body for a day or two before burying it. When he ran out of room under the crawl space, he dumped corpses in a nearby river. One he put under the kitchen floor; another, in a backyard shed.

The ghastly story began to unfold on December 11, 1978, when fifteen-year-old Robert Piest disappeared. Piest had been hired by Gacy to work on a construction crew that was remodeling a local drugstore. A few weeks later, police got a search warrant for Gacy's home. They began digging in the crawl space and in the garage. After the first three victims were found, Gacy confessed that there were many more. Piest, the killer's final victim, was found in the Des Plaines River.

After Gacy's conviction he was immediately placed on Death Row at the maximum-security Menard Correctional Center. He now claims he did not commit the murders and was convicted because of inadequate legal representation. Over the years, his attorneys have filed numerous appeals. But in the spring of 1993 the Seventh U.S. Circuit Court of Appeals rejected the latest attempt to overturn the conviction. Prosecutors say that the ruling puts Gacy within a year of execution.

Ted Bundy was put to death in Florida in January 1989. In many ways, Bundy was an enigma. Growing up in Washington State, he was a Boy Scout who had his own paper route. As an adult, the handsome six-footer was the first in his family to graduate from college. Women found him charming. His nieces and nephews adored Uncle Ted. Bundy was a counselor at a Seattle crisis center, and as an assistant director of the Seattle Crime Prevention Advisory Commission he at one time wrote a pamphlet advising women how to avoid being raped. Once, he caught a purse snatcher in a shopping mall. The governor of Washington sent him a letter of thanks.

But beneath the wholesome veneer lurked a vicious killer. Bundy was ultimately convicted of three murders in Florida and has been linked to the deaths of as many as thirty-five other young women across the country. He would usually lure young girls and women into vulnerable positions, then bludgeon them with a crowbar that he had concealed in a cast on his arm or hidden under the seat of his car. He then had sex with the unconscious or semiconscious women, usually penetrating them anally. When he was done, Bundy strangled them to death and mutilated and dismembered the bodies. Sometimes he would return to a victim's body and sexually attack the severed body parts—such as by ejaculating into a disembodied head.

Bundy murdered at least eleven women in

Seattle. He then moved on to the ski resorts of Colorado, where he killed more. Twice he was caught, but he escaped. Eventually he fled to Florida.

On January 15, 1978, Bundy entered the Chi Omega sorority house and beat and strangled Margaret Bowman and Lisa Levy, both twenty. The key evidence against him was bite marks on Levy's breast and buttocks, which the prosecution claimed could only have been made by Bundy. About a month later, twelve-year-old Kimberly Leach disappeared from her junior high school. Her decomposed body was discovered eight weeks later. Police discovered credit card receipts indicating that Bundy had spent the night before the murder nearby. They believe that Bundy suffocated the girl by shoving her face in the mud during his sexual assault.

A few days before his scheduled execution, Bundy announced he would give details of the murders for the first time. A handful of law enforcement experts flew in from around the country. Each was allotted several hours with the serial killer.

But Bundy continued the con. He revealed almost nothing.

* * *

Throughout the 1980s in Rostov Oblast, a Soviet province near the Black Sea, bodies of thirty-four young boys, girls, and women in their twenties were discovered in wooded areas. Each had been mutilated; sex organs and other body parts were missing.

Panic spread. Police pulled out all the stops, assigning hundreds of uniformed cops to patrol parks and public buildings throughout the area. The cops hoped that the killer would get nervous; now he'd have to shift to a more secluded area. At that point, undercover cops hoped to nab him.

The ruse worked. In November 1990, a police officer noticed a man emerging from the woods. He checked his identification and learned the man was Andrei Chikatilo, fifty-six. Police quickly discovered that Chikatilo's name was on a list of previous suspects. When they checked his whereabouts on the nights of several of the murders, Chikatilo's alibis didn't hold up. He was arrested.

Police questioned Andrei Chikatilo for nine days but he admitted nothing. Finally, a psychiatrist was brought in. The doctor read aloud a profile of the killer that police had put together. It said the killer was likely a middle-aged, impotent man who was experienced in winning the trust of children. Recognizing himself, Chikatilo began sobbing. He confessed. Not only did he admit to the thirty-four killings police knew about, but he told them about more than a dozen others. In all, the innocuous-looking Russian had killed and cannibalized fifty-three people over a twelve-year-period.

Chikatilo told police that he lured children or drifters into the woods with promises of anything from vodka to chewing gum. He'd knock them unconscious and stab them repeatedly while he masturbated. Later, he cut out various body parts. Sometimes he ate them.

At his trial, Chikatilo sat behind a steel cage. Relatives of his victims filled the courtroom, screaming and banging on the cage. The serial killer began each day in court by haranguing the judge incoherently. Court-appointed psychiatrists could not say whether he was faking insanity.

It didn't matter. Chikatilo was sentenced to death.

When police raided apartment 213 in a housing complex in Milwaukee, Wisconsin, in the summer of 1991 they found body parts and human skulls from eleven victims. Sitting quietly on the couch was the killer—thirty-one-year-old Jeffrey Dahmer, a pale, soft-spoken man who worked in a chocolate factory.

Police, wearing oxygen masks and protective suits, discovered three heads in Dahmer's freezer, one on the bottom shelf of the refrigerator, five stowed in a box and in a filing cabinet, and two more stashed on a closet shelf. They found five full skeletons and remains throughout the apartment—including bones in cardboard boxes and decomposed hands and a genital organ in a lobster pot—as well as bottles of acid chloroform and formaldehyde and various tools, including three electric saws.

There was no food in the apartment, only condiments. Dahmer calmly explained that he ate the bodies of his victims.

At the trial, psychiatrists portrayed Dahmer as a disturbed young man—an alcoholic and a homosexual who despised gays, as well as a convicted child molester. They pointed out that Dahmer had been sexually abused at age eight, and grew up preoccupied with death and torture. Once, as a teenager, he had skinned and gutted a dog and then mounted the carcass on a stick next to a wooden cross. His stepmother told police that Jeffrey had developed an interest in chemistry. "He liked to use acid to scrape the meat off dead animals," she said.

Dahmer began killing young men in 1985. He wasn't stopped for six years. Once, in May of 1991, he was almost caught. He had drugged a fourteen-year-old Laotian boy, Konerak Sinthasomphone, but the teenager managed to escape. Dahmer chased the naked, bleeding boy down an alley behind the apartment complex. Police were called but the boy was dazed and unable to respond. Dahmer explained that the two were homosexual lovers and had had a spat. After police left, Dahmer led Sinthasomphone into his bedroom and strangled him to death.

Dahmer was finally apprehended a few months later when another man, also drugged, was able to escape. The man flagged down a patrol car and told police that the man in apartment 213 had a big knife under his bed and was trying to kill him. When they entered the apartment, they found the horrors of Jeffrey Dahmer's murderous past.

* * *

The sordid list continues. There was David Berkowitz, the Son of Sam killer, who shot to death six people and injured seven others in New York City. And Richard Speck, convicted of murdering eight nurses in Chicago in 1966. Also, Richard Trenton Chase, the Sacramento "Vampire Killer," Atlanta child killer Wayne Williams, Charles Manson, William Heirens, Duane Samples, John Joubert, and Arthur Shawcross.

And now, Joel Rifkin, the Long Island serial killer. Earning a place on this macabre list may give the East Meadow man a perverse satisfaction.

Chapter 20

IN many ways, Joel Rifkin neatly fits the profile of a serial killer. Robert Ressler, a criminologist who worked for the FBI's Behavioral Science Unit for more than seventeen years, has been studying serial killers for decades. He was used as a model for a character in the film *The Silence of the Lambs.*

It was Ressler who coined the phrase *serial killer:* someone who kills four or more people, in different locations and circumstances, with a cooling-off period in between. During that period, premeditation and fantasy begin to build, leading to the next murder. The fantasy is often promoted by pornography, including magazines and videos.

Rifkin, Ressler says, is the typical serial killer. Most serial killers are white men between the ages of twenty-seven and thirty-five. They are outcasts and introverted, unemployed, or else work at menial jobs. They live with a single parent, usually their mothers. As far back as early childhood, they never socialized well with peers.

"There's a series of dynamics that fit in with these guys," said Ressler. "It's not all cookbook fashion but this guy certainly fits the mold."

Serial killings, Ressler says, are based on fantasies that ordinarily begin in adolescence, about ten to fifteen years before the offender begins to act them out. Over the years, fantasies drive the individual to fetish-type behavior. That may include window peeking, grabbing underwear off clotheslines, making obscene phone calls, and a fascination with pornography. It is a gradual progression toward murder. "You just don't go from a thought to an action," Ressler says. "Eventually, the human factor becomes absent. They don't appreciate the human nature of the victim. They become literally evil."

In his book, *Whoever Fights Monsters,* Ressler writes:

All the murderers we interviewed had compelling fantasies; they murdered to make happen in the real world what they had seen over and over again in their minds since childhood and adolescence. As adolescents, instead of developing normal peer-related interests and activities where they couldn't completely control what went on, the murderers retreated into sexually violent fantasies, where they could, in effect, control their world. These adolescents overcompensated for the aggression in their early lives by repeating the abuse in fantasy—but this time, with themselves as the aggressors. . . . Sexual maladjustment is at the heart of all the fantasies and the fantasies emotionally drive the murders.

The first step for Rifkin may have been his early solicitation of prostitutes. He told police that he patronized prostitutes for about thirteen years before he began killing them.

"It was a preparation—a step in the direction," Ressler asserts. "From the beginning, he was possibly thinking of tying up, killing these hookers but he wasn't ready. It was all mental at that point. He was rehearsing."

It is likely, also, that Joel Rifkin chose to kill prostitutes because he felt power over them. "Obviously if this was a functional person he wouldn't be going to prostitutes to start with," Ressler says. "These types of people usually fear relationships. Prostitutes reflect the fact that he can only deal with a woman on the basis of buying sex. A normal woman would probably frighten this guy to death."

And yet, Ressler adds, there is an overwhelming hostility for the woman who provides the sexual release. "You get a blend of hatred and sexual desire," he says. "The anger builds. Often there's sexual malfunction. He may go through the motions but the completion may be lacking. It fuses with the sexual aggression. In a blend of rage they will blame the victim for not being woman enough to help them perform. It's misdirected anger."

In his book, Ressler describes two types of serial killers: organized and disorganized.

An organized killer stalks his victims and is methodical in how he goes about his crimes. He takes pains to avoid leaving clues to his identity. Usually an organized killer is outgoing, even charming. He may be married and hold a good job. Organized killers transport bodies from the places where the victims were killed and then hide them, sometimes quite well.

The organized killer takes personal items belonging to his victims as trophies or to prevent the police from identifying the victim. In his book, Ressler writes:

> These trophies are taken for incorporation in the offender's postcrime fantasies and as acknowledgment of his accomplishments. Just as the hunter looks at the head of the bear mounted on the wall and takes satisfaction in having killed it, so the organized murderer looks at a necklace hanging in his closet to keep alive the excitement of his crime.

A disorganized killer is different. He disregards his appearance; he is sloppy and unclean. He is single; his room is likely a mess. He is incapable of staying in school or holding down a decent job. Disorganized killers have had socialization problems since childhood.

The disorganized killer is also sloppy about his crime. He may pick up a steak knife in the victim's home, plunge it into her chest, and leave it there. He does not care about fingerprints or evidence.

Writes Ressler in his book:

Part of the reason for unexpressed anger within the disorganized offender is that they are not normally handsome people. They don't appear attractive, as measured by others, and they have a very poor self-image. Disorganized offenders tend to withdraw from society, almost completely, and become loners. If they live with anyone else, chances are it will be a parent, and probably a single parent at that. No one else will be able to stomach their strange ways, so the disorganized offender is alone, possibly a recluse. Such offenders actively reject the society that has rejected them.

Joel Rifkin appears to be mixed: he was methodical in his premeditation and in transporting and hiding bodies. He kept trophies and took pains to hide his identity. But at the same time, he plainly fits the definition of a disorganized killer—his slovenly ways and antisocial behavior. He was clearly a loner, a man whose self-image was low and anger toward society strong.

For the young women he killed, it doesn't matter how Joel Rifkin is labeled. An added tragedy is that they, too, have been labeled. As prostitutes, their background has come under scrutiny. Their families are bitter; they feel that in some ways the victims have been blamed.

No doubt prostitution is an extremely perilous profession. But it is one that is born out of desperation; it draws an overwhelmingly high percentage of young female drug addicts. It is the trap of addiction that coerces the women to sell their bodies. As president of Covenant House, a New York City–based refuge for runaways, Sister Mary Rose McGeady has counseled hundreds of young prostitutes. These are desperate young women, McGeady says, who feel they have no other option.

"It's certainly not a profession they like or trust," she says. "It's hard to imagine a more vulnerable position than to be a street prostitute today. It's not surprising that somebody could kill seventeen or eighteen prostitutes and nobody noticed. Our society in general doesn't care very much about prostitutes. People have such a negative attitude toward them."

Robert Ressler agrees. He has interviewed dozens of young prostitutes in his research on serial killers. "Bad part of town. Three in the morning. Sexual contact with a stranger you don't know anything about—they're natural victims for this type of personality," he says. Many of the women, he adds, mistakenly believe they can protect themselves, that they can judge their customers. "It's the old adage: 'It won't happen to me,' " he says. "They all said they're a pretty good judge. Some of the most violent offenders are the nicest guys you ever want to talk to."

Did Joel Rifkin seem like a nice guy too? Did he chat amiably with his victims before he killed them? Did he tell them of a fictitious world—that he was Jimmy, a married man with children, as he told Charlotte Webb?

Only Joel Rifkin knows for sure what happened in his truck beginning in 1989, and he may never reveal anything more than he already has. And so it is Jeanne Rifkin who is left to explore the mystery, and challenge her doubts. For whether fairly or not, it is she who must face society's questions about the son she raised.

It is the victims' families who must endure. For them, the pain is endless. It rises with every fresh development in the case, as bits of new information are disclosed. They must fight the urge to re-create the last moments: the terror of their loved ones as they slowly and painfully died at the hands of a monster.

As the unmarked graves of these young women were at last unearthed, the families learned the truth. And then, for Joel Rifkin, the match was over, his quest for celebrity ended. Once called a loner, a loser, Joel Rifkin may now believe he has finally succeeded at something.

The man they call the Long Island serial killer has left behind a most bitter legacy.